Breakfast
on
Pluto

OTHER BOOKS BY PATRICK McCABE

FICTION

Music on Clinton Street

Carn

The Butcher Boy

The Dead School

PLAYS

Frank Pig Says Hello
(Based on *The Butcher Boy*)

CHILDREN'S STORIES

The Adventures of Shay Mouse

Patrick McCabe

Breakfast on Pluto

HarperFlamingo

An Imprint of HarperCollins*Publishers*

FIRST EDITION

Designed by Elliott Beard

ISBN 0-06-019340-9

98 99 00 01 02 ❖/HC 10 9 8 7 6 5 4 3 2 1

DO FIONÁN AGUS R

'Go anywhere,
Go anywhere without leaving your chair
and let your thoughts run free
Living within all the dreams you can spin
There is so much to see
We'll visit the stars and journey to Mars
Finding our breakfast on Pluto!'

'Breakfast on Pluto' was a UK chart hit
for Don Partridge in 1969.

Prelude

The war begins, Battle Of The Boyne,
Ireland, July 1690.
William Of Orange, with an army of some thirty-six thousand men, including English, Scots, Danes, Germans and Huguenots, met James The Second with an army mainly of French and Irish, numbering about twenty-five thousand. Despite the gallantry of Irish cavalry, James was put to flight and William was triumphant.

March 1955; Two hundred and sixty-five years later.
Into the village of Tyreelin (pop. 1500) on the southern side of the Irish border, a young boy is born.

Approximately one mile from there is a place that looks mysteriously like his but yet is a separate state, its terrain zigzagged with roads that seem to go everywhere and nowhere at all, across which cattle and bombs and butter and guns seem to travel with dizzying and bewildering rapidity. Customs officials daily have their status reduced to that of Keystone Cops when their huts are not being blown sky high, that is. Conspiracies seem to threaten the most innocuous of conversations.

Tyreelin holds many memories which our hero(ine) Mr. Patrick Pussy Braden is born with but only becomes aware of as he grows.

In 1745 a crofter was garoted.

In 1848 a landlord dragged from his bed and put to the rope.

Not long after that, twenty protestants burnt in a barn.

Xmas 1881, a Catholic man disappeared and was found in a ditch, a crucifix hammered into his head.

Dark things seemed to scurry about, always on the move.

The grey sky fretted, observing all that went on behind the brooding hills that necklaced this troubled and unsettled place, wondering with an achie in its heart: "When will it end? When will it end and peace at last enfold this hamlet so that they might be proud to call it home?"

And then—mayhem yet again, erupting from seeming normality.

1920; Dublin City in turmoil, ditch murder by the day. The country split from top to bottom.

1922; a geographical border drawn by a drunken man, every bit as tremulous and deceptive as the one which borders life and death.

Dysfunctional double-bind of border-fever, mapping out the universe into which Mr. Patrick Braden, now some years later found himself tumbled.

Distracted by the bombs and bullets, eviscerations, nightly slaughter. And ultimately deciding to devote his life to a cause and one alone. That of ending, once and for all, this ugly state of perennial limbo. To finding—finally, and for us all!—a map which might lead him to that place called home. Where all borders will ultimately vanish and perfume through Tyreelin Valley, not come sweetly drifting.

Where the dreams of Mitzi Gaynor and Vic Damone are not only attainable but float before your eyes in a land transformed by wonder. An end to abandonment, rage and lust for vengeance, the terror of galactic aloneness. Making his way—irrepressible optimist—through a terrorized London where every night might be his last, that dream of home where it might all make sense glowing like a beacon in the shuddering, siren-split night.

Such are the dreams of Paddy Pussy, transvestite prostitute, Tyreelin, Ireland, as he negotiates the minefields of this world through pastiche, wickedness and cheek.

But will it all be so easy for him, this fragile, flamboyant self-styled emissary, or shall he prove nothing more than another false prophet, ending his days in a backstreet apartment, sucking his thumb and dreaming of Mama, a silly old hopeless Norman Bates of history? Or will he triumph, making it against all the odds through the gauntlet of misfits, dodgy politicians, errant priests, psychos and sad old lovers that is his world, laying his head beneath a flower-bordered print that bears the words at last: "You're home."?

BELFAST GOOD FRIDAY 1998
The war over, now perhaps we too can take—however tentatively—those first few steps which may end unease and see us there; home, belonging and at peace.

PATRICK MCCABE

xiii

I Was a High-Class Escort Girl

Although I'm afraid I don't get too many clients these days! I can just imagine the reaction of my old acquaintances if they saw me now, sitting here in my silly old coat and head-scarf—off out that door and down London's Kilburn High Road with the lot of them, no doubt! Still, no point in complaining—after all, every beauty has to lose her looks sometime and if the gold-digging days of poor old darling poo poo puss are gone for ever, well then, so be it. I ain't gonna let it bother me, girls! Just give me Vic Damone, *South Pacific*, plus a yummy stack of magazines and I'll be happy, as once more I go leafing through the pages of *New Faces of the Fifties*, *Picturegoer*, *Screen Parade*, gaily mingling with the stars of long ago.

Old Mother Riley they call me around here, never passing up an opportunity to shout: 'How's about you, darlin'?' or 'What's the chance of a bit tonight then, Mrs Riley?' whenever they hear me coming in.

Quite what they would have to say if they suddenly become aware of just how many 'bits' the old girl has given away in her time, I would dearly love to know! Sometimes it can be hard to resist, let me tell you!—I find myself on the verge of calling back: 'Why yes! Of course, boys! I'll leave the door open tonight and you can all troop in and give me a jab! Why not!'

Shouldn't be long running then, methinks! Embarrassed-out-of-their-lives, poor little innocent red-cheeked, shovel wielding horny-handed sons of the soil of counties Sligo, Leitrim and Roscommon!

But, best that it should never come to that, for the truth is that they're all grand fellows. What benefit them, now that so many years have passed, to know the sordid, squelchy details of the life that once was lived by darling Patrick Braden—*sigh!*—sweetness pussy kit-kit, perfumed creature of the night who once the catwalks of the world did storm as flashbulbs popped and, '*Oo!*' she shrieked, '*I told you, from my best side, darling!*'

As off on the arm of Mr Dark and Broody then she trooped! Rock Solid handsome man, mysterious kind she liked. Who would bass-voiced coo: 'I love you!' and make her stomach gurgle till she'd swoon.

A Word of Advice from Dr Terence

Write it all down, Terence told me. 'Everything?' I said. 'Yes, just as it comes to you.'

It was great, him saying that. Especially when he listened so attentively to what you read, making you feel you were his one special patient and that no matter where he was or what he was doing, all you had to do was call his name and there he'd be: 'Well? And how's the scribe?'

That was what he called me—the scribe! 'Ah! There you are! How are you today, my old friend, the scribe!'

Which made his vanishing act all the harder to bear!

You wake up one morning, call out his name as usual and what do you find? There he is—gone! As they say in Tyreelin.

I won't pretend I wasn't upset. I bawled for days. 'How do you like that, then?' I said to myself. 'You certainly made a right idiot of yourself this time, Braden, Scribbling all that rubbish and thinking it would make him stay for good!'

But I mean, there's no harm in hoping. There was no harm in hoping, was there? That every morning you'd wake up and there he'd be—standing right in front of you, looking at you and smiling in that lovely way he was going to do for ever.

Just how beautiful that might have been, I certainly haven't the words to describe, despite all the supposed skills I am supposed to have in that particular field! (At school

Peepers Egan used to say: 'Braden! These essays of yours—they're absolutely wonderful! If only you'd settle down! You could be so good!')

I don't regret writing all this (in the end I put a name on it—*The Life and Times of Patrick Braden*—original, eh?) because some of it he definitely did like—I know, because he told me. 'This is terrific!' he said one day and raised his bushy eyebrows over the page. 'It really is!' And all I could think of then was don't ask me why!—him putting his arm around me and saying '*Pussy's mine! She's mine and she belongs here! With me.*' One of his favourite pieces of all and he used to keep asking me to show it to him was the bit about Whiskers although he knew that strictly speaking he should have been encouraging me not to call her that—(after all, to him she *was* my mother)—which I wouldn't have minded because for him I'd have called the old bat anything!

The Life and Times of Patrick Braden

Chapter One

Merry Christmas, Mrs Whiskers

It was a beautiful crisp Christmas morning. All across the little village which lay nestled on the southern side of the Irish border, one could sense an air of tense but pleasurable expectancy. Already the small birdies, as if conscious of the coming mood of celebration and acceptable self-indulgence which was so much a part of the much-loved season, had begun their carefully co-ordinated invasions, their industrious beaks like so many arrowheads stiletto-jabbing the frosted gold-tops of the early-morning milk bottles. Even at this early hour, there are one or two children playing—cork guns being proudly displayed and nurses' uniforms flaunted in so many minx-like parades. In places, the snow has begun to melt but this is still a scene that any seasonal greeting card would be more than proud to play host to. A door closes quietly and the first Mass-goer makes her way determinedly through the streets, her Missal clutched tightly and her knitted cap pulled firmly about her ears. Through a gap in the clouds comes the peal of a church bell. Already, the beloved pastor of this parish, Father Bernard McIvor, will be busying himself inside his sacristy. Donning the starched vestments which, it would later be the contention of an ill-informed psychiatrist, were partly responsible for his son's attraction to the airy appareil of the opposite sex.

For him, in many ways, these Christmasses have lost their meaning. Once upon a time, as a young curate, he remembered, he would have held his congregation in thrall with tales of yuletides long ago, and of the special meaning the season had for all Christians throughout the world. His homily topped off, as a plum pudding with a sprig of holly, with one of his truly awe-inspiring renditions of '*The Holy City*' or perhaps '*O Holy Night*', for which he was renowned throughout the length and breadth of the country. Or had been, once upon a time. But sadly those days were no more. When asked why he no longer sang in the church on Christmas morning, his eyes would appear to glaze over and he would regard his inquisitor with an expression of mystification almost as if the reasons were far beyond him too. Which they weren't, of course, for as many of his parishioners knew, despite rarely giving voice to it in public, the what might be termed: *Change in Father Bernard* dated back to a single 1950s morning and to no other—the morning he inserted his excitable pee pee into the vagina of a woman who was so beautiful she looked not unlike Mitzi Gaynor the well-known film star. And then arranged for her to go to London so that there would be no dreadful scandal. 'Dear, dear. I wonder what is wrong with Father Bernard,' his parishioners would say, adding: 'He's not the man he was at all.'

It would have been nice, of course, if at any time in the intervening years—particularly at Christmas—he had arrived down to the Braden household with a little present for his son. Which he didn't, of course, with the result that Yuletide celebrations in that particular establishment consisted of one plate of Brussels sprouts, a midget of a turkey and God knows how many half-human children growling and tearing at it like wild animals. And, of course, 'Mummy' sitting puffing Players in the corner, shouting. 'Quit youser fucking fighting! And 'Stop tearing the arse out of that turkey!' Santa jingle-belled all the way to the North Pole. What? On the television? Are you out of your mind? Whiskers Braden couldn't afford to buy televisions! Any jingle-belling there was took place on the beat-up old wireless on the mantlepiece above our dazzling array of wee-wee-stenching undies.

But nevertheless all's well that ends well and now that she's suitably drunk she decides to pull the only cracker available, triumphantly producing it from her handbag and yowling: 'Come on over here and pull this fucking cracker till we get this fucking Christmas finished with!' as, happy family that we are, like a snapshot from the past, we all come crowding around, happy bright-eyed bastards all—Wee Tony, Hughie, Peter, Josie, Caroline and snot-trailing Little Ba, who for such a magnificent display of domestic harmony are hereby presented unopposed with the Patrick Braden ALL-IRELAND FUNCTIONAL FAMILY OF THE CENTURY AWARD! So congratulations, Hairy Ma and all your little out-of-wedlock kids!

Chapter Two

Patrick Braden, Aged 13 — The Trouble Begins in Earnest!

Peepers Egan, the English teacher and acting headmaster, was on the verge of losing his mind as he paced the floor of Class 2A, St. Martin's Secondary School, Tyreelin, intermittently smacking the sheaf of papers with the back of his weatherbeaten hand as he addressed his hangdog pupil: 'How dare you!' he croaked perplexedly. 'How dare you submit the like of this to me, Braden! When I said it would please me if you would develop your literary skills, I did not—I repeat *not*! (his croak quite high-pitched now)—mean this!'

It was unfortunate that I had now learned the truth once and for all about my clerical parentage (Whiskers having blabbed it one drunken evening), for I really was becoming quite obsessed with it. Wasn't deaf to the whispers about town when I'd go walking past, either! Hence the persistently colourful titles of my submitted essays, e.g., '*Father Stalk Sticks It In*' and '*Father Bernard Rides Again!*'

It was inevitable, of course, on foot of this, that poor old Peepers would have to come down and visit Hairy Ma.

It was his duty, after all, and, I daresay, the execution of which probably came close to putting the poor man in his grave. 'You see, Mrs Braden' was all you could hear as he twisted and turned in his chair. 'I have to be seen to do something . . . it's a direct challenge to our authority and a slur on the character of . . .'

'Daddy!', I almost squeaked.

But didn't—keeping my own counsel very impressively indeed right until the very end when Peepers said: 'You won't do it again, will you, Patrick? You'll try and stop this anti-social behaviour. You'll try and fit in, won't you?' when I replied: 'Oh, no. I haven't the slightest intention of stopping it, Peeps, or trying to fit in either!'

It was, in fact, impertinent of me to call him that. 'Peeps,' I mean. Because he *was* my teacher and I liked him and should have shown him more respect. An appraisal of the situation with which Hairy hastily concurred, out of nowhere landed a fat-fingered thump on my jaw, squealing: 'Don't talk like that to the Master! He's a cur! From the day and hour I took him in off the street, Mr Egan, a cur!'

Understandably, Peeps didn't want to get involved any further for he'd gotten himself into such a state about everything already that I think all he wanted to do was charge off to the Tyreelin Arms and have himself a few dozen whiskies.

Chapter Three

In Flagrante Delicto, 7.03 p.m., Sept 13, 1968

I was absolutely sure I was safe, you see, I really was, having cocked my ear to the bedroom door for at least five minutes and then at last heard them squawk: 'Hello, Patrick! Patrick—yoo hoo! Are you up there at your books? Me and Caroline are off to Benediction now!' before trooping off down the hall and closing the front door behind them. 'Gone for at least an hour!' I cried, in the grip of a delightful excitement. But no! Hardly twenty minutes later—the pair of them back, mooching about the kitchen looking for a prayerbook or something they'd left behind. None of which I was aware of, of course, being much too busy dabbing on Whiskers' lipstick (Cutex Coral Pink, would you believe!) and saying: 'Hello, Patricia!' into the mirror and pretending I was dancing with Efrem Zimbalist Junior!

Whom I didn't really know, of course, except that I'd seen him in *Modern Screen* once or twice and really liked the look of him—thought the name quite fab too, may I add! And was more than glad to say: 'Oh yes!' when he husky-groaned: 'Like to dance then, sweet Patricia?'

As round and round we twirled to my favourite song: '*Son of a Preacher Man*'—what else, darlings!—with Efrem crooning, 'The only one who could ever teach me was the____' at exactly the same moment as the door came bursting in (they must have heard me '*la-la-laa-ing*'!) and who's there only—yes!—Caroline going: 'My dress! He's wearing my favourite dress!' and putting on quite a performance, I have to say—(Watch out, Efrem! This is Oscar material we're dealing with here!)—as Whiskers gets a grip of me and starts yowling and—*slapping* me, would you believe!—saying that this is it, this is definitely the end—and then, can you believe it, collapsing hopelessly into tears!

Chapter Four

Mrs O'Hare's Smalls

A situation which wasn't helped, I admit it, and it's not something I'm proud of, by my promising that I would never do it again because they were Caroline's private things and I had no business taking them, and then sneaking off a few days later and dealing Mrs O'Hare's smalls off the washing line, pretending this time that I was dancing with Lorne Greene out of *Bonanza*! Why him, don't ask me, whether it was the distinguished grey hair or what I don't know, all I know is that someone had seen me climbing over the fence into her garden and next thing there's O'Hare in the kitchen waving her fists and shouting about the guards. It was stupid, of course—I mean you can imagine what I looked like in those voluminous monstrosities! (O'Hare was huge!) But I was so frustrated—dying to dance with Efrem so much that I couldn't get it out of my mind!

Predictably enough, it didn't take long for word to get around the town and all you could hear going up the street was 'Ooh! Cheeky!' and 'Lovely boy!' It was pointless explaining to them that I wasn't at all that interested in sex and that all I wanted was for Lorne or Efrem to say to me:

14

You see this spread? It's all yours. Your name's going on the door, Patrick! It's all yours from now on!

Some nights I'd lie there thinking about that and then see—don't ask me why!—Caroline and Whiskers standing outside in the rain, drenched, asking: 'Can we come in?'

Whereupon I'd chuckle a bit and shrug as I looked at them and said: 'Sorry, folks! Closed, I'm afraid!'

Well, poor old Whiskers! Would she be furious about that or what!

Chapter Five

Welcome to Juke Box Jury!

Certain other people, however, would be admitted straight away to my salubrious abode, and in would stomp to marvel: 'Boy, Braden! What a place!' as I cried out: 'Hellay, dahlings! To my castle, welcome, old friends Irwin Kerr and Charlie!', continuing to make up more posh rubbish for them to join in with—why? Because that was the way we went on and always had. For as long as I could remember they'd been calling down to Rat Trap Mansions, annoying the arse off Whiskers asking her could I come out to play cowboys and war. I met Irwin first when he was in mourning for his brother who was eaten in the Congo by Balubas. He was in floods of tears coming across the square, choking: 'Bastards! Fucking bastards!' and saying every one of them would have to die. Except that only three days later, his brother arrived back from Africa with an ebony elephant for everyone in the street and not a bother on him from the day he'd gone off with his kit bag. 'He *was* in a fight but . . .', Irwin said, as we headed off the next day to our hut, which was the headquarters of the famous Kane Gang. 'Even though I'm a girl, I have to be in charge,' Charlie said, 'Otherwise you can forget about the whole thing.'

Me and Irwin didn't care who was leader. All we wanted to do was read her comics and listen to the records she played on the battery-operated record player her sister brought home from England. We'd just sit there on the grass, clicking our fingers and going: 'Fantastic! Fab! It's just fab, baby!'

That was how the international modelling shows started. Charlie would bring out her mother's clothes and start showing all these magnificent creations to fashion-buyers and pop-star managers from all over the world. 'What do you think?', she'd say, and I'd frown and cradle my chin as I said: 'Oo! Magnifique!' or 'No! I do not like it!' in the same French accent.

The Juke Box Jury Shows just grew out of that, I suppose, and before long there was one every day. As soon as we got out of school, we'd race off out to the hut and get our gear on and Charlie would go behind the plank which was the juke box jury counter and announce: 'Ladies and gentlemen! You're welcome to Juke Box Jury!'

In the beginning, she did some singing too but after a while I did most of it because Irwin said he was too shy and so there I'd be, going: 'You know you make me wanna shout!' or 'Stop! In the name of love!' by the Supremes as Charlie held up her cards and cried, like the woman on the telly: 'I'll give it foive!', as Irwin shouted: 'It's bollocks. It's a load of bollocks! Look at Braden the eejit dressed up as a woman!'

Which I rarely was, to be honest with you—although not from lack of desire!—and made do mostly with a pearl necklace or one of Charlie's mother's blouses. Still—it was better than nothing! And sometimes she'd bring out a perfume spray to squirt all around the hut and make it smell just fabulous! 'Nothing like perfume for taking all your cares away!', I'd say and do a twirl. 'If this doesn't stop,' Irwin said, 'I'm quitting the gang!', but Charlie said: 'Oh pipe down, why don't you,' and he did, shuffling off and sticking up two swear-sign fingers.

It wasn't long after that anyway that we started the wars as well and that kept him happy, there wasn't a word out of him about the perfume and the international modelling as long as we promised to keep doing the wars. Which I didn't mind in the slightest, especially as Charlie clicked her heels and went: 'Compan-ee-tenshun!' I loved that, for some reason—her being the boss! As off we'd march behind her, and shout 'Die, dog!', as he stuck his bayonet in their necks.

How all that started was that 1966 was the jubilee commemoration of the 1916 rising and no matter where you went in Tyreelin, everyone was waving a tricoloured flag or singing an Irish ballad. Every day there was a different politician in the town and in the pubs at night they were all talking about getting into a lorry and driving across the border to take over the north.

To tell you the truth, we didn't care that much for the wars in the end. But Irwin—he was going clean mad over them! He had even taken to wearing his James Connolly rebel hat around the town and going off over the fields on his own to practise drilling. To keep him happy, we kept on saying the wars were great and then running off back to the hut to put on the Beatles and go absolutely mad as we clicked our fingers and jived in and out among the sheep and cows, singing: 'Try to see it my way! Do I have to keep on talking till I can't go on! We can work it out! We can work it out!' until we couldn't do any more and just lay down there holding hands and staring up at the sky. And which we kept on doing, and had no intention of stopping, right through secondary school and everything!

Chapter Six

Most Popular Adolescent Boy

Which at times must have been difficult for Charlie, for let's face it, what with the famous 'smalls' and other similar episodes which I shan't bother going into here, as time went on, it became abundantly clear that I wasn't exactly growing up to become Mr 'Most Popular Adolescent Boy' around the town! Not that it seemed to bother her, mind you! 'Oh, who cares, Braden!' she said, 'The sooner they blow this kip up and be done with it, the better!'

Something that—now that we were a bit older and had started noticing these things—didn't look like it was going to take very long at all, for every time you picked up a paper, someone else had been shot or maimed for life. Of no consequence to me, of course, for, as I said to Charlie, I really wouldn't be hanging around for very much longer. 'You're fucking right,' she said. 'And as soon as I get my exams, I'm gone too!'

Charlie was doing her Intermediate Certificate Examinations now and I was in my final year at St Fucky Good-for-Nothing's. Herself and Irwin were the only people I could be remotely bothered with. 'You're out of your mind!' Irwin said. 'Breaking into shops to steal cosmetics! You're a Head-the-Ball, Braden!'

'Indeed,' I said. 'No doubt your Provisional IRA friends will be around to short me out!'

'Don't worry your head about the Provies!' he said. 'The Provisional IRA have a lot more to do than be bothered with dying-looking bastards the likes of you, Braden!'

Chapter Seven

A <u>Real</u> Soldier and a Work of Art Delivered

Quite how Irwin even managed to get around to conceiving of himself as a real soldier really must be classified amongst the great unsolved mysteries of our time, for the silly little idiot wouldn't have been able to shoot a crow! But now, of course, nothing could stop him, it being 1971 and with the balloon in Northern Ireland having gone up in earnest, it was his bounden duty and his chance at last a *real* soldier to become, to take up arms and: 'Fuck anyone who gets in the way!' He really was hilarious when he got started!

I, of course, was much too preoccupied with my own personal revolution to be bothered with anything so trivial. As my dearest father was soon to discover when, having made my decision to once and for all to take my leave of sweet Tyreelin, I decided to pop in his letterbox one of my more recent (hopelessly obsessive—of that let there be no doubt!) and exhaustively crafted compositions!

Chapter Eight

Breakfast Is Served

'Ah, God bless us, it's yourself!' remarked randy old Father Bernard on a grand soft day in February as he opened the door to reveal the young girl who—despite her dowdy appareil, the clergyman reflected silently, and not a little wistfully—bore a startling resemblance to a very well-known film star standing on the front step of his residence. 'It is indeed,' replied the young girl. Who, on account of her coming to work for the local parish priest had—acting upon her mother's perlexing advice—gone out of her way to take precautions and camouflage herself—with the result that (at least *she* felt!) she looked just like any old ordinary priest's housekeeper you might see shuffling along the road with her shopping basket or ferrying a plate of rashers and eggs across the floor to her employer. And most definitely *not* a perfume-sprayed vision called Mitzi Gaynor with a head of gorgeous bubble-cut curls that would make any man's privates go—*sprong!*—never mind that of a poor deprived clergyman! (Young Eily knowing nothing of all this, of course!)

In spite of her inexperience, the clergyman's new employee found herself to be quite relaxed about the position she was about to take up, her situation rendered much less intimidating than it might have been because of the fact that in those times, almost as if there was a church employed quartermaster somewhere to whom one could apply for the standard uniform, one had no difficulty whatsoever in acquiring a washed-out,* pale blue housecoat with a ringpull zip, a pair of tan stockings the colour of tea kept in the cup for twenty years or thereabouts and an old hairnet which when you squashed your hair under it made it look like irregular handfuls of rabbit's droppings. All of which served the purpose for which it was intended of saying to the little penises of all those whose duty it was to bend the knee and wear black serge: 'No mickies today! Off with you and say your prayers for no tiddler stands for girls like these!' Callous as it might now sound, inserting one's wee man into these rasher-frying ladies—well, it simply wasn't on! You couldn't do it, dearies! 'Go in!', you'd cry to Peter but I ask you—could you do it?

Let us consider for a moment that melancholy sound which, at crucial moments in the world of animated cartoons is often to be heard: after so much labour and literally lakes of perspiration, all the efforts of Tom the woebegone pussycat have all but come to naught—no, *have* in fact, and here he is, his entire body corrugated from head to toe, bludgeoned, his tattered soul in disarray—only—despite the fact that he thinks nothing further of an adverse nature can possibly befall him—to find that a large anvil has

*Not entirely unlike my own!

appeared above him, making its way towards him at great speed, all the better his poor bewildered head to flatten. What is that sound upon which we now attend, appropriate to this dicky downward-going moment so familiar to house-keeper-retaining clerics all across the land? Why, three groaning notes upon a cello played—*waugh! waugh! waugh!*—as flump goes Mr Prawn the dicky-doodle man!

Or so perhaps was hoped! But what if this is not the case and inside those black pants a riot is about to start? No! It simply cannot be! Mickey is devious, mickey is naughty, but drab old housecoats, shuffly slippers and stockings of cold tea must surely ensure he minds his manners and stays where he belongs.

Which is exactly what our hero thinks. And goes on thinking it right through his breakfast, the contents of which he is consuming with great gusto, pausing intermit-tently to magnaminously observe: 'God, but them's great sausages altogether!' and 'I'd do jail for another slice of that fried bread!', thinking to himself all the while just how lucky he is to have found a replacement as good as this for Mrs McGlynn who had become indisposed at such short notice. 'Ah, Mrs McGlynn,' said Father Ben, 'God love her! Slipped and fell outside Pat McCrudden's gate!' as he advances upon a crispy slice of yummy bacon with his fork, smiling away contentedly to himself.

His new housekeeper is thrilled by all this of course! As indeed, why wouldn't she be? After all—this extra money will be buying not only Perry Como's latest record but also perhaps—if Mrs McGlynn ('God forgive me!' she whispers softly) stays out sick for long enough—the complete, long playing soundtrack of *South Pacific!* You could hardly believe that in an ordinary, unspectacular presbytery in a small village in Ireland that no one had ever heard of, that the sun could rise and singing angels practically fill the air when someone thinks of such a little thing, but in that moment that is almost what did happen: on her first morning in his kitchen, Father Bernard McIvor's new housekeeper flapping her arms and in her mind skipping along the sand with a straw hat on her head and Rosanno Brazzi calling after her 'Wait for me! Wait for me, you silly girl!'

What might have happened if she had not leaned, for no reason other than to fork some more rashers onto Father Bernard's plate—thereby permitting her housecoat and skirt to ride up just a little, not a lot, but just enough—must remain forever in the realm of conjecture. Was she herself aware of the fast-moving developments occasioned by this oversight on her part—the mental suspender of a white girdle gleaming in the gritty sunlight—why, of course she was! Which was why she remarked: 'Oops! My skirt and housecoat are riding up! Better about this task at once or we could have an explosive clergyman filling the air with pent-up sexual energy thanks to God knows how many years' abstinence!'

O yes—but of course she said that! I mean—what else would you expect? Because, like Father Bernard, thwacking penises and salty sweatbeads running down your face were never off her mind! Well, excuse me, Father, but don't make me laugh—please don't make me fucking laugh—you know? For that sort of thing she doesn't think, actually. That sort of thing she doesn't say. She doesn't fucking care, you see!

Rosanno say: 'Darling?' and kiss her full on the lips? Of

course, Frank Sinatra in a nightclub tilt his hat and croon to her alone? Yes! And yes a million times! But trembling, veined stalks so invasive, angry? I really do not think so, Father! I really do not fucking think so!

But to Father Stalk—as he shall thenceforth be known— such considerations were immensely academic, of course. As Mr Mickey in his fury now reminded him. Tick tick goes time bomb in the parlour. 'Oo!' he cries—old Mick Micks— 'would you look at that! Not often you see a foot of thigh so creamy in this place we call the presbytery, is it, Father? It certainly is not! By golly! Is this a surprise or what!'

As indeed it was and could not be denied. But nothing— absolutely nothing—when compared to the one experienced by the merrily-humming help in the housecoat when, through the air, out of the corner of her eye, she perceived what she took to be a flying man: (*Newsflash! Priest grows wings in latest miracle!*) and was about to giggle: 'Gosh, Father! How did you do that!' when she found herself enveloped by her own skirts in the manner of a parachutist who has just effected one of the most unsuccessful jumps in the history of aviation. At first, she really was one hundred per cent certain that it was a joke (albeit, it has to be admitted, one a little more daring and outre than one might expect from the store of Father Ben, who, as a rule, contented himself with stories along the lines of '*Peanuts at Confession*'—in which the confessor asks the penitent boy: 'And did you throw peanuts in the river too?', only to receive the side-splitting hilarious reply: 'No, Father, I *am* Peanuts!' (It was one of his favourite stories and he rarely missed an opportunity to tell it when he and his colleagues were relaxing at conferences and so forth.) But—she thought it a joke nonetheless! Which made her go: 'Oh, now, Father!' and 'Eek!' and 'Oops! That hurt!' until all of a sudden she cried: 'Ow! I'm being split in two!' and there was so much squirty stuff all down her she thought that maybe Father Ben was playing more games—squidgies with the Fairy Liquid washing-up bottle that she'd often seen the kiddies doing. It was only when he fell back across the room with a Hallowe'en mask on him that she really became confused, thinking to herself: 'But it's not Hallowe'en!' How long it was before she realised that it was in fact her Employer's actual face she was looking at—and not a whey-coloured Egyptian mummy-type papier mâché affair—is impossible to say but she eventually did, realizing too that the Fairy Liquid—it wasn't Fairy Liquid at all! And that thing—that glaring red thing with its malevolent eye—what was that?

You see, in those days girls didn't really have any experience of boys and their electric little tootling flutes! To be perfectly honest, I don't think they even knew they had them. (And their mammies weren't going to tell them! 'Don't ask questions now, Eily!', Mrs Bergin had said as she knotted her daughter's drab old headscarf!) To them, what was between a boy's legs was a little snail-type fellow your brothers had. Not an insatiable, unreasonable trunk of a thing that reminded you of some illogical version of the song that you heard regularly on the radio, except now going:

> It was a one-eyed, one-horned flying purple
> weenie-poker
> One-eyed one-horned flying purple weenie-
> poker!

28

Instead of the correct words. And who would obviously stop at nothing now until he had you destroyed with sticky stabs and practically broken you in two into a bargain! All she could think of as she lay there on the table with the small moist map forming on the fabric of her housecoat was: 'Rosanno wouldn't do it!' and 'Neither would Vic Damone!' (Whom she also loved.)

All of which made her break down in tears—and is it any surprise! Why, it was as if into the spoon of a ballista she'd been placed and unto the outer reaches of space propelled!

Are you aware, dearest Papa, that did from nothing spring me—but mysteriously has forgotten!—that a song telling of all this once was sung, echoing out across the birdcalling day as beneath the skies once more we did entwine, a girl called Charlie Kane and me? 'Go any-where,' we sang, Daddy, 'Go anywhere without leaving your chair/ and let your thoughts run free/ Living within all the dreams you can spin/ We'll visit the stars and jour-ney to Mars/ Finding our breakfast on Pluto!'

It's a beautiful song, isn't it, Father? You can be a dan-delion seed floating out across with the world when you hear a song like that.

Do you think that was what she was and she laughed all the way out there on her own, Daddy? A dandelion seed in a happy childhood song?

No—you're right, daddy—she wasn't.

And all because of you! All because of naughty Papa who should never have left his chair to do his naughty wander-ing! Isn't that so, Daddy? Don't you think that's true, when you think about it—*Father*-of-the Year?

Chapter Nine

Ladies and Gentlemen— Mr Dummy Teat!

I know it's not nice—or healthy, either, maybe!—wanting so badly to see Daddy's face when he opened those elaborate letters of mine (Yes! There were others! Quite a prolific author I turned out to be, Peeps!) but I just couldn't help it. Whether or not he had words with Hairy I don't know but after having furnished his postbox with a series of blistering specials ('Sex Mad Sky Pilot!', 'Fornicator', 'The Adventures of Father Benny Rape!', etc.) I decided it was time once and for all to vacate Rat Trap Mansions.

Well—can you believe it! No sooner have I said, 'I'm going,' than Caroline and Whiskers are on top of me, pulling at my jacket and going: 'You can't! You Can't', doing their damnedest to get me to reconsider, after spending years threatening to turf me out themselves! 'Please, Paddy!' was all you could hear out of Caroline, 'What will you do—where will you go?' and Hairy shouting: 'Let him go! Let him go to hell! What do we care! We're better off without him!', and then changing her mind and offering to be nicer to me—even offering to give me money when I was leaving! (Which of course I willingly accepted as I had been entitled to it all along, considering the amount the government and, as it transpired, on the quiet, old Father Stalk, had been giving her.) And was probably the only reason she wanted me to stay at all!

In the end, anyway, none of it made any difference in the wide world as off I went with my little bag, my coat thrown across my shoulders, strolling along the gnat-infested country roads on the way to Scotsfield, the next nearest town, with my thumb stuck out, although not caring a damn whether or not a car stopped now or in ten days' time! I was free! 'Birds of the air—as free as you!' I chirped and burst into a song by Gilbert O'Sullivan. Why? Don't ask me! Just as—*screech!*—I couldn't believe it, a Merc pulls up beside me and who is there as the door swings open but the one and only, ladies and gentlemen—His Eminence Mr Dummy Teat! My darling Married Policician Man!

What I didn't know, of course, was that no sooner than I'd left the house, Whiskers had gone off down to the police station to get the guards out after me, who, if they had found me and saw what I was at now, making eyes at good old Dummy in the front seat of his car, would have had plenty to say about it! Not that I cared what they had, for now my journey had begun and I could tell by Dummy as he hungrily chewed his bottom lip that he, for one, about that would have no complaints to lodge!

The great thing about old Dummy was that with him you just didn't know what to expect. All you could say with any degree of certainty was that at any hour of the day or night, that old tootling stick he had in his trousers would always be ready for action. 'Oh, man dear, he's at it again!' he'd say,

and you'd have to, as he said—'Put him out of his misery!'
Yes, I will make no bones about it, post Leaving Certificate
in the bomb exploding year of 1971, I was more than content to be the regular partner of my new benefactor in the
warm and toasty cosiness of his perfumed Merc. So clean in
there! Which, I have to admit, was the first thing I really
liked about Dums. Sweat? Stale pee? I really do not think so!
The very embodiment of hygiene and good manners! O but
of course I understand that there were many who would
impugn his good name—importing arms for the IRA and
any amount of old nonsense!—but, whether the truth or
not, the fact is I don't care and didn't, for never once did I
have to nag or gripe. Never once in all my time with him as
lover husband, call him what you will, did I ever smell old
yukky sweat or see some grime between two toes. Why, after
Rat Trap Mansions, Stench Capital of the world, I must have
died and gone to heaven, I thought each day that I woke up!
And all thanks to my darling Dums, this loving man of a
thousand potions. Just how many brands of aftershave did
he use? It must have run into two figures.

'How do I smell?', he'd say to me and I'd reply: 'Just
fine!' lots of the time not paying the slightest attention at
all, of course, besotted with some shoes he'd bought me
(or should I say—*I* bought with *his* money—for he really
didn't have a clue about girl's things!) or spraying on
some Chanel No. 5. (You see, he didn't care! 'Have what
you want!' he kept on saying. 'Shag the fucking cost') O
he was a dreamboat, that old Dummy Teat!

But that tootling stick with which he poked—it definitely
was a problem. 'You really will have to leave me alone, you
know. I simply am exhausted!', I'd try my best to tell him.

32

Always, sadly, to no avail. 'Give me another little chuck chuck!' he'd say then, or 'How about a little tune for Dummy?' Then—off I'd go, down on my knees and crooning away—but not for fun-time jollies only! O no! Sometimes, my Dums, so serious he could be. 'You sweet and darling beauty! How much can I give you to make you mine for ever?'

Well, obviously I couldn't be his girl into perpetuity but I was quite prepared, if he continued to lavish me with compliments and cash, certainly to remain with him for as long as—well, who knew!—and would indeed most likely that have done, if he hadn't gone and died. I often think of him, blown up like that, his poor little mickey in slo-mo coming back to earth, like a flower pink and bruised, an emblem sent by all the dead men who'd crossed over. There are those who say it was the IRA and others the protestant Ulster Defence Association and then some who say it was the two of them together. I didn't know, and didn't fucking care. All I knew was that dear old Dums was gone! Poor old Dummy! Why did you have to immerse yourself in the sinister world of double dealing? Why, you and me, to this day we could have been together!

Obviously, I knew he was on edge about something. At nights I'd take his tootling stick and say: 'Please let me, honey. Tell me all your secret troubles.' But he never would. He'd just shed a tear and sigh, then touch me, saying: 'No! Then they'd only come for you!'

It was something to do with guns and the money it cost to buy them. Every time I think of them shovelling him up with spades it's like wire chucked tight in my chest. I loved the cottage he'd put me in. It had belonged to his mother.

'I miss her so, my mother,' he'd say. 'Never a day goes by but I think of her, that lovely woman.' That was why I started calling him Dummy. Of course it wasn't his real name! Who ever heard of a politician called that! *Well, ladies and gentleman! That's quite enough from me here this evening! Now, with your permission, I'd like to hand you over to the man of the moment—Mr Dummy Teat!'*

Very likely indeed. No, his real name was much more ordinary than that and I'd tell it to you only I have better things to do than get myself blown up again, thank you very much—anyway, it isn't really of any consequence. What I can tell you is how Dummy came about. Because it was me who put it on him, that silliest name of all!

'Oh, Mammy!' he'd say when he got in one of his moods and I came up with this ideal of inserting my thumb into his mouth. It was quite a spontaneous gesture on my part—but, oh boy, did he love it! 'Oh, Mammy! Mammy!' he'd cry, sucking away on it like nobody's business! I can't *tell* you the states he used to get into when I'd flutter my lashes and say—actually, not even say, but mime it—the word 'Dummy'.

He just could not get enough of it! Once he got so excited that afterwards he handed me three hundred pounds and said: 'Here—go on! Buy yourself whatever you like, you teasy little brasser you!'

Chapter Ten

A Dublin Interlude

Now one moment, Dummy, I'm sorry but I really will have to stop you there, for you know very well how much I do not like to be called a brasser—'Peachy', 'Yum Yum', even 'Little Horny'—yes! But 'brasser'—it simply shall not be tolerated! What am I then, darling? A Dublin fishwife in tattered nylons, holding up a doorway with a fag-end on her lip?

Dearest Dums—I really do not think so! But I shall relieve you of three hundred crisp ones and off to the city now I swoosh, with Charlie Kane-Patchouli by my side ('How can you bear to put it on you, Sweetness!') in her battered bearskin coat and suede purple inset flares she'd bought in the Dandelion.

In which Dublin market place, all our Saturdays we allowed them to waft away. A cloth Indian belt and nature shoes—I simply gave up in despair. ('What are you doing, Charlie? Are you out of your mind! Don't waste your money on such ugly, horrible things!') As meanwhile, courtesy of the Dummy Teat Financial Institute, my arms I filled with Max Factor, Johnson's Baby Oil, Blinkers eye-shadow, Oil of Ulay, Silvikrin Alpine Herb shampoo, Eau de toilette, body moisturizers, body washes, cleansing milks, St Laurent Eye and Lip make-up, Noxene Skin Cream and Cover Girl Professional Mascara. Not to mention clothes! Knitted tops in white, purple, lavender, blazing orange, satin-stripe velveteen pants, turtle-necked leotards, flouncing skirts, ribbed stretch-nylon tights. 'Haven't you got enough, for fuck's sake?' said Charlie, but I thought I had only started! Is it any wonder that she never fell for me?

'Please kiss it,' I begged her, oh, so many times. 'My one-eyed, one-horned, purple people-poking Peter,' but she just laughed and said: 'No! Why should I! When all you want is the impossible—a vagina all of your own!' And to that—what could I possibly say when it was true.

*

In St Stephen's Green in Dublin, there is a shop called Trash. Well, not now there isn't perhaps! But in January 1972 there was! 'O Trash! We love you!', we both chirruped in time! And why ought not we both to love, adore it, when a belted sweater in yummy plum to match your crushed velvet hot pants could be purchased for a snip? Except that, snip or no, we could have purchased them anyhow! 'O I love you, Dummy Teat,' I cried and Charlie cautioned: 'Ssh now!' She said I was the talk of the place. 'You don't mean they know about Dummy?' I said. 'Of course they know!', my sweetness replied. 'The whole country does—both north and south!' To that what could I say but: 'Gosh! Oh, no!'—but intention of leaving him, this girl had none! 'We really must buy you a wig of your own!', she said—and did I look a dream in that Schiaparelli ('Pretty, wash-and-dryable and impervious to heat'—but cost an absolute fortune!) No matter, as dear Dummy said, why those bouncy, high-gloss curls when coloured with an ash-brown *Tried and True* haircoloring—they were worth all the money in the Allied Irish Bank! 'Do you love me, Dummy?' I simpered and would those peepers answer: 'Yes! Pretend you're Audrey again!', he said—(We'd gone to see a special double bill in Castleblaney—*Breakfast at Tiffany's* and *Roman Holiday*!), and then I'd go, 'Oh Gregory!' with the coyest flap of a white-gloved hand. 'Phew!' he'd say then when we'd finished. 'I'll tell you one thing—it would be a while before my wife would pretend she was her!' Meaning Audrey, of course!

In Grafton Street, the following week, who did we run into only Irwin. Who we'd been seeing less and less of—now that I was living in Scotsfield and he was so busy going to meetings and selling his republican papers. 'So—where are you off to, Kerr?' we said. 'I'm on an anti-internment march,' he said. 'What? That is it?' I said. 'Well—*quite* a crowd!'—which I shouldn't have said because things like that could drive him crazy! 'Less than a fucking hundred people!', he hissed—as if we were personally responsible. 'The south doesn't give a fuck!' 'O leave it,' said Charlie. 'Come on with us and drown your sorrows!'

And which he did! Immersing himself in the giantest Coke float in Captain America's of that very same old Grafton Street. I like it, looking back on that day we met Irwin, talking more rubbish as usual. 'The only fucking band worth their salt right now are King Crimson, Charlie!' he said, blowing Cokey bubbles. 'All this glam-rock—it's a load of shit!' With which I certainly did not concur—but not so much for the music's sake as the clothes! 'You

37

mean you don't like Ziggy?', Charlie said and curled her lip. 'You're out of your fucking mind!'

I lost interest after a while and started going dreamy. There was a nice song playing on the jukebox. It was *'Rocket Man'* by Elton John. More than a little ironic when you considered the life Irwin was leading now, for you could see by the way he talked that he was in quite deep politically. Half the time I didn't hear: 'This time we're going to finish it! Or 'Stiff the whole fucking lot of them! You got me?'. And I felt like saying: 'O for heaven's sake, Irwin! Cop yourself on! Let's live a little first and leave the rockets to the guys who enjoy it!'

And—secretly—thought: 'In other words, those who shall never know the pleasure to be gleaned from prettying one's hair or making-up one's eyes!'

At which I was definitely now becoming adept, disporting myself in glam-rock satin jackets and unspectacular denim (ugh!) jeans but *still* attracting attention. Effortlessly gathering compliments: 'Look at him! He's wearing womens' clothes!', 'Jasus! Look at that!', and other assorted idiocies! 'Your're getting fucking worse!' said Irwin when I twirled and asked him, 'Well—you like the pink or blue?' meaning yet *another* satin jacket!

After Captain America's I got my hair done and Irwin said I was the spit of David Cassidy. I have to say that I was flattered! Then it was off down the street with cans of Harp, Irwin in that silly shirt with the great big fist bursting through a chain: '*Smash Internment Now!*'

Quite how it happened, to this day I'm afraid I still can't say—all I know is that I was a little tiddly, dawdling and sleepily (the cans of Harp, I'm afraid) fingering the gypsy cut strings the hairdresser'd clipped and was paying absolutely no attention to them—actually shocked in a way when I looked up and saw then both embracing—Irwin with his tongue halfway down Charlie's throat, in fact! The foggy mystery right then for me was: How can you suddenly fall in love when you've known one another for years and years? Well, you can, I'm afraid.

'Why! Your face—it's gone quite flushed, soldier!' I cried when the comrade re-emerged. 'Does your fancy man kiss you like that, you crazy fucking nancy boy?' he said and hit me quite a thump. 'Please!' I said and demanded: 'Let's go get more Harp!'

By the time we got home—ten more Harps on the bus— I was so tiddly that I just about knew my own name. 'Paddy Pussy, dahling!' I had decided to say to anyone who happened to cross my path. 'At your service, deah! How can I help you, you behstud? Not only 'intended', but in fact— actually *did!*

And to a British soldier, of all people! 'Name, please?'— *'Why, Paddy Pussy, dahling!'*

Not a very good idea! Especially when we got home and heard thirteen people had been shot dead by British Army paratroopers in Derry. I was absolutely mortified, and not feeling quite so tough then, I can tell you!

It all having, as you can imagine, the opposite effect on Irwin. 'Steady on! Steady on for fuck's sake, Irwin!' was all I could hear Charlie saying as I sat with them in the darkened square, shamefully not thinking about the dead victims or their relatives but what combination of my luscious goodies I should go and try on first!

Chapter Eleven

Hysterical Jokes and Greeting Visitors in a Skyblue Negligee!

When Dummy was at work, I'd spend my time reading magazines—*Loving, True Confessions* ('I was a bedroom tease! My man was hooked on a hooker!')—thinking to myself how if I did somehow manage to get a vagina, one thing I was certain of, and I didn't care even who it was with, was that I wanted at least ten of a family. I know some women nowadays would say: 'Pussy Braden! You're out of your mind! You are out of your fucking tiny mind! Do you know, do you for one second know, what it would be like looking after that number of people?' To which I could only say that I do and probably if the truth be told, probably know it a lot more than feminists or anyone else who might hold those views. You can just imagine it, lying there on your deathbed, the cancer or whatever it is, literally rampaging through you, and, from every corner of the world, in aeroplanes, ships, long-distance trains, all the children for whom, through thick and thin, you have broken your back, together now braving the elements, withdrawing savings, fighting bitterly with employers, simply in order to be by your side. And there you are, with your lank and tired hair, a few bad teeth perhaps but behind your eyes, that thing they know, and always have, which through this life sustained them, the thing we all call love. 'Always you used to say to us, Mammy,' they'd say, 'like tooth and nail together fight but outside stick together! Do you remember that, Mammy?' And would I remember it?

My eyelids closing in a gesture of recognition—a small smile playing upon my lips. So many there with all their partners, each one of them of Mammy proud. *'Who will love them for me?'* was a question I once had asked, when I dreamed of being from this world gone early. And now, I had my answer. Everyone would my children love for they themselves knew love and shared it. It would be sad, of course it would. But a happiness there would be too, perhaps even close to ecstasy. As all about me now they gathered and I heard their tender whispers: 'Do you remember the little picture we had above the fire? With that sweet, entwining blossom and the words that read: "*Chez Nous*"?'

And then once more, for the very last time I'd smile. Smile and whisper if I could: 'Of course, my darling. Of course, my beautiful, lovely darlings!'—each one of them from my hard stomach labours so lovingly sprung.

And who would ever to deny it dare? To say: 'They are not hers! For she has no vagina!'

There would be no one. And as my eyelids slowly closed and the first tears pressed their way into the world, I'd clasp each hand and say goodbye, to each adieu bid, safe in the knowledge that baby one and baby two, right up to baby ten, had all their lives been given it, and to the very end received it, that wonderful thing called love.

Could it ever have been? With my own dear Dummy? Methinks it not! That great big blazing fire and me with my arms around my knees and my head resting on his thigh, going all misty and wondering: 'Dummy? Where do you think we'll be in twenty years' time?' as he stroked my hair and said: 'Huh?'

Poor old Dummy! He really didn't have the life of a dog with me, did he? One minute I'm there as black and broody as ever a woman could be, pulling away from him and going: 'Oh, get your hands off me! You'll never under- stand!' and the next I'm gone all woozy, like never until the end of time will I leave this lovely man. Which may or may not have been true—I genuinely couldn't say—for who's to know whether 'like' can someday be 'love', become that something special over years? And 'like' him I certainly did. He was a lovely companion, no matter what lies they told about him in the papers! And I'll tell you something else about him—no matter what they'd been through or what- ever terrible things she had said about me and our relation- ship, I never heard him once speak ill of his wife. Not that I wouldn't have welcomed the odd 'old cow!' or even 'jealous bitch!', to tell you the truth! But it was never to be forth- coming. 'She has a generous heart, she really has,' he'd say and I admired him for it.

Although I have to say there was little evidence of this so-called generous heart the day she came around slan- dering me in front of the whole countryside. Not that I didn't understand, mind you! If I was married to someone and *they* went off with somebody, I wouldn't just shout a few words of abuse. I'd make their lives miserable, if you want to know the truth! Everywhere they went, they'd find me there—and not the nice, well-groomed, soft-spoken version either! The wicked, cast-hissing one, more like, harridan of all harridans who would think absolutely nothing at all of tearing your clothes or cutting your face with a few well-aimed scratches of her polished nails! You don't think I would have it in me? Well I'm afraid you don't know me, at least the *me* where love is concerned! I go absolutely crazy even *thinking* about someone taking the one I loved away from me.

Which is one of the reasons I didn't bother going to his funeral. How was I to know, what with all the stress and the strain and everything, Mrs Faircroft—(the Mrs)—might spot me then and lose control of herself the way it's possible to do after bereavements, heap all the upset and hurt on top of some poor unfortunate individual, a relative you've had differences with or whatever. I simply wouldn't have been able to withstand that, everyone looking at me and going 'Do you see him . . .' and all this rubbish, whispering away as usual.

Which, as I say, was all they ever did about me and Eamon. (Yes! That's him!) To tell you the truth, I don't think they were actually capable of understanding us in real, sort of concrete terms, if you know what I mean—I don't think they could accept that it could ever be!

So in the end I though the best solution was to just not go. I sent a Mass card all right—deep down, he was a very religious man, no matter what they said about corruption and murder and all the rest of it. But I thought it better not to sign my name. I just put down, '*A friend.*'

A few nights later in Mulvey's, they said to me: 'You know where they found your boyfriend? One half of him in Tyreelin parish and the other half in Clonboyne!' This was supposed to be the joke of the century, of course. Another night, I was going to the toilet when one of them squeezed my arm and said: 'How did they know Eamon Faircroft had dandruff?' I shrugged—not that it made any difference whether I did or not because I was going to be treated to the hysterical answer anyway: 'Because they found his head and shoulders in the river!'

Well, excuse me, darlings, while I wet myself.

Not long after that, I had a visit from the IRA and I was caught in flagrante delicto again, doing myself up at the mirror. 'I'm in for it now!' I thought to myself. I mean you try talking to flak-jacketed men in ski-masks wearing only a hairnet and skyblue negligee! I threw myself against the wall as they came in and cried: 'Go on—do it then! Murder me! But please—*please* make it quick!'

'Oh, shut up, Pussy!' one of them said and straight away, I recognized him as McGarvey from Tyreelin Cross. I tried to get my own back on him—he never stopped wolf whistling when he saw me coming down the street—by making up all sorts of lies when he started asking me questions. By the time I finished poor old Dummy had been working for the Mafia, the CIA and Interpol all at the same time. 'You needn't be trying any of your fairy tales on us, Pussy!' one of them said then and they all laughed. I nearly laughed myself, to tell you the truth, it was so absurd—me standing there in my Doris Day outfit raving about poor old Dums and international espionage. They were wasting their time, of course, as I kept on telling them, for they found nothing and in the end they just said: 'Ah, fuck this!' and cleared off. Making sure to give me a nip on the backside as they went, plus—surprise, surprise!—a rousing chorus of '*See you later, honky tonk!*', which was the latest around the town—thanks to Dick Emery and that stupid TV show of his!

If things had improved even a little bit, I think I might have considered staying around Tyreelin for another while but if you look at those first six months of 1972, you would have to ask: 'What person in their right mind who had a choice would stay *five minutes* in the fucking kip!'

Especially if they've just gone and lost themselves a lover, and most likely soon to be chucked out of house and home? I think what put the tin hat on it was when they decided to top young Laurence Feely. After that, I was off—for sure!— and wild horses wouldn't have dragged me back.

Chapter Twelve

Celebrity Squares

Laurence, being Down's syndrome, couldn't pronounce his words right—which was why I called him Laurence Lebrity. No matter how he tried he just couldn't get it right, the name of his favourite programme—*Celebrity Squares*. I used to meet him every day and say: 'I suppose you'll be watching it tonight, will you, Laurence?', and he'd start clapping his hands and jumping up and down. Quite what he must have made of two completely strange men standing in his living room while he was watching Bob Monkhouse reading from his cue cards, all you can say is God only knows. Nothing, I suppose. Too busy clapping his hands and going: 'Lebrity Kwares! Lebrity Kwares!'

When they started asking him the questions, most likely he thought it was his own sort of private *Celebrity Squares*. And why, probably, he raced up the stairs so enthusiastically to get his rosary beads when they leaned in close and asked him, smiling: 'What religion are you?'

Which they were happy to accept as an answer, and why, after they had raped his mother, they put the beads around his neck like a garland and said: 'Clap your hands for *Celebrity Squares!*' which he did, as enthusiastically as ever.

It think it was the first Down's syndrome boy shot in the Northern Ireland war. The first in Tyreelin, anyway.

Chapter Thirteen

A Girl Who Knows She's Loved!

How flattered I was by the attentions of a certain gentleman, I really cannot impress enough upon you, and, had one not at the deepest level possible by recent deaths been so affected, they might well have been a determining factor in overturning the decision alluded to earlier—the leaving of Tyreelin town!

Once, to my little cottage, I received an anonymous letter, doused with powder and, secreted within, in elegant script, the words: 'I love you—you know me.'

Which I did, of course—because, could Jojo Finn stay anonymous to save his life? Of course not, the great big idiot, shuffling about in his denim bomber jacket, peering out of the shadows—completely besotted, I'm afraid it would appear! All I can say is—thank heaven Eamon didn't apprehend his missive! There would have been one hell of a row!

Which is not to say I wasn't flattered by the nervous affections of my suitor full-of-longing. I most certainly was! Especially since they were responsible for his presence in the Sports Centre dancehall that fateful night in Cavan! When Pussy got her make-up smudged!

What happened was we decided on the spur of the moment to hit Cavan to see the Plattermen—Irwin was crazy about them. 'You want to hear their version of *"With a Little Help from My Friends"*—Joe Cocker doesn't have a smell!' he said as his battered Anglia motored into Cavan. Later falling about the street he roared at little bins: 'The Free State's either with us or against us! Anyone else thinks different—stay out of the fucking way!' Charlie stood up on the steps of the courthouse and flung back her batik scarf as she informed bewildered citizens that she wanted to 'Paint two thousand dead birds crucified on a background of night', stuffing her book *The Mersey Sound* back into her pocket as off we went then to the care, to encounter—mysteriously ensconced in the corner, now in silk scarf and tartan jacket, and puffing on his smokes—sweet lover Jojo Finn!

As I sipped my coffee, throughout from Jojo those furtive glances sailing. Stop it, Jojo! You're embarrassing me! But honest question! Did it stop me preening? It most certainly did not! I couldn't stop thinking: 'He's all dressed up tonight is it for me? I wonder what he thinks of me in my skinny rib and two-tone flares!' Not to mention my gorgeous brass hoop earrings! Which all Cavan had stopped with cries of: 'He's wearing weemen's earrings!' To which I replied: 'Affirmative, darling sweety-pie!'

Charlie—not so discreetly sipping from a vodka bottle — now appeared upon the table singing Yes songs at the top of her voice. 'If the summer change to winter, yours is no disgrace! Yours is no disgrace!', she yowled into the microphone-bottle, shaking her backside and swishing her bearskin coat to reveal her jeans and smiley faces, felt pen scribbles: Black Sabbath, Peace and Love—Clapton is God. Melty-eyed Irwin ate a handful of chips and gave me the peace sign. 'Wait till you hear him on the bass. Rob Strong is a fucking genius, man—I'm telling you!' Across the town the Plattermen started off the dance with a piledriving Afro-Cuban number. As Irwin joined Charlie on the table and they both took the bottle-mike for Santana's *'Oye Como Va!'*, managing ten whole seconds before the Italian owner cam running with a screech—as Jojo's eyes at last met mine and did his face go—*whoosh!*

*

How the dancehall fight started I haven't the faintest idea, to be honest with you! I do seem to remember someone pulling my sleeve and enquiring as to my gender. After that, all I remember is: '*Skree!*', and the women losing their minds as the bikers tried to get a kick at me. You can picture the scene, I'm sure—leather jackets, hefty boots and 'Kill the hooring nancy queen!' As out of nowhere comes a vision! Jojo! I can't believe my eyes! My not-so-secret admirer with fists now squared and, lit with drink, ready to tackle them, one by one!

'Leave him alone! Fucking leave him alone! He's a Tyreelin man!'

Did he beat them up, each and every one? Well—not quite! Though definitely managed to scare them away! And then does what? Goes all coy and slinks away—as if suddenly a stranger!

Except not to me, by a long shot—no! Old Puss a favour just does not forget!

'Come back!' I called after him. 'Jojo!' Adding, in a whisper—'Darling.'

'What happened?' Irwin squeaked, coming up for air—some soldier! (It was Jojo the IRA should have recruited—not him!)

As through the streets I then did wander, searching for that heart of mine—Jojo Sweetness, saviour of his girly! Running him to earth in the alleyway by the New Pin Cleaners, my heart skipping a beat and, truly, little tears coming misting to my eyes as his hand I took, not a word between us whispered as I touched it—so cold and sweaty—fearful?—and nibbled gently on his earlobe. 'Thank you so much,' I murmured and mascared eyelashes permitted droop a little. How could he be so afraid?

'It's OK, Jojo. It's OK, pet!' I said and then was gone, a kiss blown back across the night now quiet. Along with three mimed and simple words: '*I love you.*'

'Where the fuck were you? We were searching everywhere for you!' bawled Irwin Smash-the-State when I got back. Charlie was reading *The Mersey Sound* to a telegraph pole.

'Oh, nowhere, Irwin, honey!' I beamed, utterly consumed by the proud, exquisite, giddy tremor of a girl who knows she's loved!

Chapter Fourteen

A Head on Him Like
Barney Gillis's Cockerel

It was an ordinary midweek afternoon in early summer in the town of Tyreelin. Eamon Faircroft had been dead some months now and already time had begun its healing work on the soul of Patrick Pussy. Obviously he would never forget the man with whom he had spent such a short but beautiful time, occasionally, as he sat there on the summer seat, feeling the corners of his mouth begin to twitch and behind his eyes a little glitter-twinkle started as he recalled some joke that Eamon had told him, or an idiosyncratic story they had shared on the way to Enniskillen where they dined out every Sunday. Was it any wonder poor Puss was sad?

Especially when he was unceremoniously thrown out of his abode, fag-puffing workmen hammering planks across the door as Puss she weepily waved goodbye.

'What you're doing, you'll never know!', she said. 'The memories this place holds!'

'Oh, fuck off, Mrs Braden,' bawled one of them and chased him with a plank.

'In trouble again?' laughed Pat McGrane (old classmate) as he pulled up his Anglia, on his way across the border.

''Fraid so, Pat!' simpered a tattered Puss, 'So where might you be off to then?'

'Off to Armagh to see the missus!', said Pat with a grin.

'I didn't think she was the missus yet', said Puss.

'She's not', replied Pat, tossing back his black shoulder-length hair, 'But it'll not be long now!'

'Well for your Sandra', said Puss, 'Wish someone'd marry me!'

'Don't worry!', said Pat, as off he went tooting his horn, Creedence Clearwater Revival blasting from the tape deck, 'Don't worry, Pussy—one day they will! Keep on choogling now—you hear me now?'

'I do, John Fogerty! I do!', called Puss as Pat's hair flew out into the wind.

*

Fortunately, for all the time that remained to her, good neighbours came to the rescue and now she sat with Charlie's folks in front of the television watching David Bowie and the Spiders From Mars cavorting in their unitards.

'Ah, for the love of Christ!' Mr Kane said. 'Did you ever see the like of it? For Jasus' sake—I ask you!'

Mrs Kane went out to put on the kettle and called from the kitchen: 'Oh, you needn't be asking me. It's that pair there you'd want to ask.'

He shook the paper and vanished behind it, Bowie pouting on his knees.

'The cut of the cunt—arsing about my television with a head on him like Barney Gillis's cockerel!'

Whereupon we took our leave upstairs where Charlie's Salon was now in progress, Alice Cooper blasting through the open window. 'Lift your head, why don't you,' she said. 'I can't get at your neck!', foundation dab-dab-dabbing with her cotton ball.

'You look fantastic!' she said when she was finished. 'I could eat you!'

And then: 'I'm going to miss you, Pat Puss, you know! So much.'

'I love you, Charlie. I'll write every day, I promise.'

'Kiss me! Even if I'm Irwin's and always will be for ever, I still want you to kiss me!'

Yummy breasts of all time as little tongue goes travelling down to belly-town! And other secret places!

Such squelch and sweat the world had never seen! God!—why couldst not invent a sweeter way to melt and merge? Dickies which might squirt Chanel, or weenies which secrete rosewater? O who can ever tell you your plan! But Charlie—with her it was so close to exultation, one almost didn't want to go!

Hold the front page! *Pussy changes mind! Refuses to emigrate after all! Decides to settle down with long-time friend from childhood!* But it was not to be and when the time came I felt like Ingrid Bergman. 'We may never meet again, Charlie, you know that?' I wept. 'Oh, shut up, Braden!' she snapped and, moist-eyed, hugged me yet again. 'Please don't say it for I love you so!'

'Good luck then, Head-the-Ball,' said Irwin.

I was sorry to leave old Irwin too, standing there with his red hair and freckle-splashed face. Under his arm a pile of papers: *Republican News.*

'I can't get around him, Patrick!' Charlie said. 'He's off his fucking head!'

As purring bus went *vroom!* And *whoosh!*—away we go!

Chapter Fifteen

Elephants to England

'I boxed for Kilkenny—I boxed for Ireland!' said the man with the scalded prawn face. 'And I'd be boxing yet only for my accident!'

How sad that it transpired they had put him in prison—for offences unnamed. The lights of Liverpool yet far away as *The Munster* ferry made its way through the churning waters. What is that I discern just below the eye of Boxing Man Extraordinary? Why I do believe it's a nervous tic!

'You're a funny class of a buck!' he says. 'Dressed like that . . . would you not be afraid . . . ?'

I was sporting a scarf of purple chiffon, ever so decadently aflutter.

'Why, darling?', I said and moved ever so slightly closer.

Now who would have expected a pugilist and a saucy Pussy to be in the lifeboats so entwined?

'Elephants they call me,' he said as he indulged in his post-coital smoke. 'If anyone lays a paw on you—just tell them Elephants isn't far away. I'll bate them! I bate more men! I'd batter them!'

'O Elephants!', I sighed.

Then what does he do—start to cry!

'I hated prison!' he says. 'It did all sorts of things to me.'

As after a good sobbing session, off we went down to the bar where '*A Nation Once Again*' was in full swing. I felt sorry for Elephants with a nose like that, beaconing over the rim of his pint. His eyes begged: 'Could you love me?' Well, I could—but I had a lot of things on hand and it really would have to wait. I shouldn't have stolen money out of his pocket as he snoozed there on the booze-splashed table. But he had promised me a tenner and there wasn't much sign of it coming!

When I went up on deck, the air was sharp and clear and the dawn was beginning to come up. I leaned over the railing and sucked in the salt breeze. Strung all along the coastline, they set my soul atingle, winking: 'Hello there, Puss!' at me, each one glistening through the fog, the lovely lights of Liverpool.

Suddenly—An Expert!

I'm well aware of course that a lot of people might say—certainly Terence said it often enough—that while I seem to have had no problem sympathizing with Charlie's tragedy (she had a breakdown not long after Irwin was murdered—but we'll go into that later) there appears to be no similar generosity of spirit evident when it comes to my treatment of Father Bernard. Who—Terence kept coming back to this—must have been tormented, not only by my persistently vindictive missives but by the sight of me strutting about town in the ostentatious manner I did. 'I mean—we are talking about a small, enclosed village here,' Terence said. Now suddenly he's an expert on Irish rural life—after me telling him everything he knew! Before that, he wouldn't have known where to look in the atlas—for Ireland, never mind Tyreelin!

Chapter Sixteen

In a Pig's Ear, Sweety-Pie!

But he's right, of course. I mean—I supose I did turkey-hen around the place a little, crushed velvet purple loon pants one minute, baby pink satin jacket and stackheeled glitter boots the next! 'After all,' he said, 'one could hardly expect the poor priest to invite you up to the presbytery and say: "Sit down there, son, and have a cup of tea like a good fellow. Myself and yourself have a lot to catch up on! By the way—I love the powder blue, puff-sleeved shirt—or is it a blouse? Ha ha!"'

All of which is fair and reasonable enough, I suppose. But I wasn't bothered about any big speeches or get-togethers like that. All I wanted him to do was say: 'Hello there, Patrick,' once in a while. Even nod, for heaven's sake! But he couldn't even do that much! As a matter of fact, any time he saw that I was sitting on the summer seat, he put his head down and made a detour around by the back of the chicken-shed. Did I mention that ever since I'd been dumped on the front step of Rat Trap Mansions I suspected Whiskers had been getting extra cash for my upkeep, over and above what the government gave her? ('Mickey money,' they called that locally.) Well—she was! For definite! From good old Father

59

Bernard, believe it or not! And, to be fair, when all's said and done, at least they can't take that away from him! Only Caroline let it slip one time she came to visit me in Charlie's, I might never have found out. I was furious and stormed off down to the house straight away!

'How dare you!' I said to Whiskers. 'Cheating me out of my rightful inheritance! I could have you in court! You realize that! Don't you!' then what does she do only start to blubber. Caroline too, of course! Then next thing I look out the window and who's there staring and noseying in—O'Hare! I flung the window open and shouted: 'What are you looking at? Think I'm going to steal your bloomers again, do you? Well, you needn't worry! I don't need your old drawers! I was in a right fury, I can tell you! I was especially sorry because Caroline's boyfriend Frank arrived right in the middle of it and was mortified.

I mean—I was chucking things around and everything! I have to say that I really felt especially sorry for Caroline—because when I was living with Dummy, she used to bring me food and money. (As if I needed it—I was loaded! But I couldn't tell her that!)

'What's to become of us, Paddy?' she said sometimes and seemed so genuine. I even embraced her once, when she was leaving—I swear to God!

And now, here she was with her new boyfriend—he was a lovely fellow—Frank from the bank I called him—having to listen to me! 'You could have fucking told me!' I said. 'You could have given me something! But no! All you ever gave me, all you ever handed down was the smell of piss and clothes nobody ever bothered to wash! Thanks a bunch! Thanks a whole pile, fucking Whiskers!' I hadn't meant to call her that. On the way over, I had said to myself: 'Don't call her that now. Whatever you do, don't call her that, it isn't fair'. And now, here I was, doing it. 'Fucking Whiskers!', I said again. Once or twice, Frank tried to calm me down but I'm afraid I wasn't taking any of that from him. I mean, at the end of the day it was our family. 'Fuck off, Frank!' I said. 'You don't know what it was like! What it was like being reared by a thief! How would you possibly know!'

Bad and all as it was, practically destroying the kitchen (which really looked quite nice now that Frank and Caroline spent a lot of time in it, keeping it clean and what have you), it really made me feel an awful lot better and by the time I had calmed down I was able to say to Whiskers: 'I'm sorry. But it really did upset me when I heard it.' Unfortunately, nothing I could say or do could placate her and she was still blubbering when I left. But Frank and Caroline left me to the door and would you believe—actually offered me twenty pounds! Which I said I couldn't take. I did? In a pig's ear, sweety-pie!

'Thanks, Frank,' I said and held Caroline in my arms. It was lovely giving her just a little peck on the cheek. 'I wish we could have done that a bit more often,' I said and she began to cry. There was no doubt about it but she was a really good-looking girl now—quite beautiful in fact. 'You're a lucky man, Frank,' I said and gave him a big grin. Then off I went. I really was quite lightheaded after my outburst.

Chapter Seventeen

I Work Here

But am still not quite sure how I ended up in the church! I'd just about had it, I suppose! Fortunately there weren't too many worshippers in the vicinity. I could imagine what they'd have to say. 'What's he doing here? He never darkens the door!' Which is a darned blooming cheek when you think about it, for if I, Tyreelin's only genuine son-of-a-preacher-man, haven't the right to be about the place then who, just who, I would like to know, has? I was as giddy as a goat as I swept through the doors and I am ashamed to have to admit there was a distinct whiff of B.O. emanating from the regions of my armpits. 'Oh, dear,' I said to myself—don't ask me why! Guess Who was on the cross as usual. Looking down to say: 'Ah, Paddy.' 'Ah, Paddy, what?' I said and shook my head. What was He *on* about? As long as I could remember, there He had been with His crown of thorns, just hanging there, ah this, ah that, ah what. That was the question I had been meaning to ask Him. 'Ah what? Ah *what*?' So I asked Him. 'What are you *aahing* about?' I said.

Like I say I was lightheaded and in no humour for waiting but fortunately just then the door of the confession box opened and in I went. '*The Holy Family's Flight into Egypt*', said the pamphlet. I rolled it up in a ball and threw it away. Just then he drew the shutter back. 'Hello, Daddy,' I said as I knelt down in the dark and you can imagine the shock I get when it wasn't him. All I could see was this baby fellow hardly older than myself looking at me through the grille. 'What are you doing here?' I said. 'I work here,' he says, as I began to realize just what an idiot I'd made of myself!

By then I didn't care though because, to tell you the truth, after the row with Whiskers I was exhausted. 'Bye bye, Father,' I said as the confessional door clicked shut behind me, 'Ah's' eyes following me, wondering, I suppose, what He'd been drinking the day he went and made a twilight zone of a disaster like me.

Chapter Eighteen

'Look! She's Lost Again!'

Well, how many times did I manage to get myself lost in that old London town—don't ask me! After leaving Euston station, I must have walked the square mile half a dozen times—each time ending up back at Gower Street. Bright-red Pussy! Thinking all of London town's ten million people are saying: 'Look! It's *her*! She's lost again!'

It was a miracle I found my way to Piccadilly Circus at all, there at last to begin my trade. (I had read about it in *Weekend* magazine—'Nocturnal Vice! The Boys Who Ply Their Trade by Night! Sins of the City That Never Sleeps!') Sounds just like me!, I thought.

Although I would have given it a lot more consideration if I'd known of the likes of Silky String—only my fifth or sixth customer, for heaven's sake! ('Ah' getting His own back on me maybe!)

Chapter Nineteen

Theme from 'A Summer Place'

'Cold, Isn't it?', I said and put my hand on his leg. 'You remind me of someone,' he says then, with this great big charming smile that would make you think: 'I've met a right old Cary Grant here and no mistake,' and the pair of us racking our brains to find out who this remind-person is. And who does it turn out to be—the one and only David Cassidy! 'That's what I should call you,' he says. 'My little David. My little David Cassidy.' I didn't ask him what his name was, because unless it was going to go further and he was going to do a sugar daddy and set me up in flat as his kitten, I didn't really see the point. Which I would dearly have loved him to do, let me add, for it would have suited me down to the ground. An English verson of Eamon Faircroft was just what I needed right in those early England days of '73 and let there be no denying it. Exactly the very thoughts going through my mind as we zoomed off through the night-time streets of London—THE BODY REVUE '72! NON-STOP AVANT-GARDE NAKED SPECTACULAR! GODSPELL! PYJAMA TOPS! 5TH GREAT YEAR! SWINGING STEWARDESSES! TECHNIQUES OF LOVE!—'I wonder what he works at now, this latest pick-up chappie of mine?' One thing I was glad of—he was certainly a lot better turned out than some of my previous customers! Absolutely appalling having to deal with some of them it was! 'And you talk about the dirty Irish!' I said to one of them. His fingernails! You wouldn't believe them! 'Dirt! I farking love it!' he says. 'Fuck me in the dirtiest place imaginable—squeal like a pig, I will!' Not with me he wouldn't!

As I said to Silky—which he wasn't called then, of course!—moving a little bit closer to him, and organising a little nose-crinkling: 'You're nice!'

'You really think so?', he says then. And I nod. Simply because it was true. Neat suit, steel-grey hair and not a single speck of dirt on his fingernails. Or anywhere else for that matter. 'Do you like music?' he says, then I said: 'Yes. Oh, yes. I absolutely adore music.' Then he looks at me and smiles. 'Wonderful. So do I. So already we have something in common.' I have to tell you—I was really beginning to like Silky. And when it was Vic Damone and '*Stay With Me*' that came over the airwaves just then—well! I must have jumped a little or shrieked perhaps, because he started laughing and said: 'You like that, don't you?' as I dropped my eyes and replied: 'Yes.'

'Quite old-fashioned for a boy your age, aren't you?'—to which I once more eagerly replied: 'Oh, yes!'

'So that's another thing we have in common!' he said, and gave my thigh a little squeeze. 'For I love Vic Damone.'

As we sped along that night—going north but of course I didn't know that then, I hadn't the faintest clue!—I just cannot describe how happy I was! All of a sudden I seemed to see the inhabitants of Tyreelin, all massed there in the square between the creamery and the petrol pumps, obligingly leaning forward, the better for me to inspect their individual features.

'Remember us?' they said but what could I honestly do only shake my head? 'Sorry,' I said and were they sad. But, as I told them, 'That's life! We all now must move on!'

'Yes! True love!' Silky was saying. 'That's what we're all after! And Vic—boy does that man know how to sing about it. You reckon, my little friend?'

'I reckon,' I said, all huggy-warm.

'And Nat King Cole. "*The Girl From Ipanema*"—hmm?'

'Mm,' I purred.

'You that little girl? You a little girl from Ipanema maybe?

We laughed.

'It's so lovely to have met you,' he says then and looks at me all glittery-eyed.

When I look back on it, I really have to hand it to Silks. To listen to him you would have thought he was the sort of person who started drenching the place with tears anytime anything remotely upsetting came on the cinema screen, for whom the abuse of a dumb animal was a tragedy of awesome proportions. Which perhaps it was of course! Just because you get a kick out of strangling people doesn't mean that another side of you can't be humane and kind and sensitive—perhaps even more so indeed.

In any case, that was all I saw in him as on we cruised with Vic still singing and the whole warm London night surging in through the open window. Crayon neon all about the jiggy-sparked inside! With swells of emotion that went right through you as you thought: 'At the end of this journey, something special is going to happen. My new lover is going to pull the handbrake and when we look out the window we will see something that will look like a shining light. Then he'll just turn to me and say: 'We've reached it. We're home.'

Which he did—turn to me, I mean—just as soon as he pulled the handbrake. But it wasn't to say anything about love or home, I'm afraid! Although at first I thought it was, because his eyes seemed to have something close to deep affection in them, which made me feel real yummy. Especially when he said again: 'So you like Vic?'

'Oh, yes!' I replied. 'I really like him.'

'Why?' he said and my first inclination was to chuckle because we both knew why, but then because it was so exciting just thinking about it again, I sort of shivered and closed my eyes as words just wriggled out of me and I said: 'Because he knows so well what it's like to be in love and what it can do to two people, when they're just dancing there and everyone's gone home and all you can hear is the sound of the city night as it slips now towards the dawn . . .'

'Take off your clothes,' he said then and I have to confess the abruptness of it did take me aback a little. But I took them off anyway, as neatly and decorously as I could—because that was what he wanted: ('Take them off—but not in a vulgar way,' he said)—and laid them on the seat beside me. Did I say he liked that? He couldn't take his eyes off them—that little pile of clothesies sitting there (Oxfam glam-rock cast-off Department, Oxford Street, I'm afraid! O how my fortunes had changed! But which were about to improve—I knew it! For without a doubt my new-found friend would give me lots and lots of cash with which to take myself to Biba's fab boutique, there to pick and choose with glee!) And was about that particular development—re: fortunes!—Sweet Puss soon proved right! But not for the better, deary! For no sooner had I my gold chain removed and my long brown hair tossed back than he had slipped his hand in his pocket and removed his silky string—although if it was indeed from that fabric fashioned, I could not say for sure. All I can accurately state is that it was a ligature of some sort, soft but not so when about your Adam's apple it's drawn tight as it will go. For some reason, at that precise moment, when he began to strangle me, I saw Charlie standing there tossing back her scarf and going: 'I want to read you a poem. It's by Adrian Henri from Liverpool. It goes like this: "I want to paint two thousand dead birds crucified on a background of night . . . "'

As I'm sure you can imagine—each and every one of those silly birds I saw as Silky String pulled tight. 'So you believe in love?', he was saying—hammering away at his tootle now, of course, into the bargain! 'So you believe in true love, then—true fucking love? Well—let's have some of that! Let's have some true love, then—true fucking love, let's have it!' He released me for a moment to turn up the music—the theme from 'A Summer Place' now, would you believe!—and it was now playing so loud I cannot understand how someone didn't hear or see us. I suppose he knew the area well—I can remember Hammersmith Bridge in the distance, but was obviously some sort of disused industrial estate—and he knew what he would and wouldn't be able to get away with. With the little bit of sight that was left to me in those bulging eyes, there seemed to be a dump outside the window. I could have sworn a seagull walked past on top of it. But then maybe that was one of Charlie's imaginary birds. 'All the things I'm going to paint,' she said, as Silky forced his tongue inside my mouth. The music was absolutely deafening now and why a passing snatch of *South Pacific* came into my mind just at the precise moment, to this day I do not know why but it did and then—the moment in fact he twisted that stupid fucking string around my neck again—it *really* was Mitzi Gaynor who was coming across those airwaves and perhaps because it seemed so beautiful and pure, it made me feel ashamed. It was as if she was standing there on the beach with her hair pinned back and her hands on her hips going: 'Patrick—why?' How I managed to get a grip of his ear I have no idea but once I did I sank my teeth into the flesh as hard as I could. What made getting away easier was the fact, of course, that his other organ was still pronging away.

In my mind I called to Charlie: 'You want to paint: "One blood-pumping liar crucified against a background of refuse!"' Which was what he was now, yelping as he stumbled out of the car, howling: 'You fucking Irish bitch! I'll murder you! You facking Irish facking filth! My eyes! I'm facking blinded!'

Which was lies—he wasn't blinded. I hadn't connected properly with my nails.

What on earth they must have thought, poor drivers, looking out through their windscreens to see me pulling on my clothes in the middle of a motorway, with the eyes still bulging out of my head. All I was worried about was that it was going to turn out like horror stories where you leave one madman and climb into a car with Mr Nicey who's going to save you—except it transpires he's madder than the first one!

70

Fortunately, however, it didn't turn out like that. He was as nice as pie, the driver, all concerned—and even drove me to the hospital. Except as soon as he dropped me off, I ran like fuck away out of there when it occurred to me they would probably ask me lots of questions like: 'Where do you work?' For some reason I just don't think: 'The Meat Rack, Piccadilly Circus' was the sort of thing they liked to hear!

As it happened, my injuries turned out not to be all that serious—except for the shock, I have to say! Why, for days after it, I didn't know whether my legs were made of string or straw or what. One thing for sure—they were not made of flesh! I felt so high I could have reached up and popped a planet or two into my pocket. My feet—one minute twelve inches long, the next expanding half the length of the street, for heaven's sake! I'd be walking along, just whistling to myself and all of a sudden I'd see him—Silky! Like some eerie version of Robert Redford, standing staring into a shop window or checking his watch before jumping into a taxi. I'd have been running for over half an hour before it would occur to me: 'Perhaps it wasn't Silky after all!' I would really like to be able to say that, like everything else, time began to pass and eventually my wounds healed. But, I'm afraid, getting throttled by the likes of Silky is not something you get over quite so easy. Particularly when you have to go on earning your living and are afraid every time some too-tle-merchant puts his lips to your ear or says, 'I love you!' it's just a pretext and very shortly you will find yourself lying on a dump somewhere. To give you some idea—before I took up my position at the railings opposite Eros, I was a little over nine stone in weight—and by the time two months' hard work at my post had elapsed, I was barely over seven! I began to give serious consideration to the possibility that one day I might at those very railings simply expire and that the end of it all would be! Much of this I attribute to police harassment, of course—not forgetting my old friends the IRA. I was really beginning to get fed up with them and their antics. For now, a night never seemed to pass without: '*Clear the area! We would appeal to you to clear the area!*' And then— 'Do you have ID? Let's 'ave a look at you, Pat!' Look you up and down then, winking at their mates, giving you the old mince mince, hand-on-the-hip routine. 'Lots of little fairy boys like you back home then, Pat! Not just murdering bombers then, after all!'

With which you could not remonstrate, otherwise lose your job!

P. BRADEN, PICCADILLY ESCORT SERVICES
CLOSED UNTIL FURTHER NOTICE

But it was sad. There could be no doubt about it. Once, an hour's tooling in a parked car in Great Portland Street just about ended, again it came a-crackling: '*Clear the area! Please clear the area!*' But it was too late, and although I arrived just for the end of it, it still was very like you'd imagine the end of the world to be. A beacon on an ambulance revolved blue as the trollied dead were ferried out and a woman in some tattered rags kept laughing at a joke. Except nobody was telling her one. 'Look at me! Look at me in my rags!' she kept saying. Radios were spitting like fat in a frier and on the telly we could see ourselves. The end of the world starring P. Pussy and all of

England. How many bodies, I really couldn't say. 'String 'em up, the Irish cants, each and every farking one of 'em!', I heard a voice beside me say.

I liked to sit in the all-night cafés because it would keep you warm and with luck you might find business. On nights like that, you couldn't taste the coffee. You'd just be feeling like dog's dirt upon a pavement, with well-dressed people standing over it and going: 'Who on earth left that horrible mess there?'

Some weeks after the business with Silky, I was sitting there in my usual place, staring out into the night with its Clockwork Orange gangs and skinheads and hippy dealers falling in and out of Ward's pub and the theatres disgorging themselves and the SKOL sign flashing on and off when all of a sudden I realised that I could smell myself! And it wasn't just the smell of dog dirt—it was the smell of a dysentery-ridden mongrel. No matter how I tried to dispel it, it still kept getting stronger. It became so foul it utterly swamped me. 'You're going to spill that coffee, mate,' the owner said to me and it was only then I realised there was a little puddle of it all over the formica, tickling in small drops on to my stinky, balding velvet loons.

Chapter Twenty

Where the Fuck Is My Mammy?

It was in there I met my darling Berts—O yummy Bertie, I love you so, do it to me again!—although what took him in there only God in His heaven will ever know! I mean, it was the type of place where all sorts of night-time flotsam and jetsam made their way—including many countrymen of my own, but most definitely not chiffon-sporting Pussies!—who would while away the hours crushing cans of Holsten and alternating between blowing up England and vowing that they didn't agree with the deaths of civilians. Then they'd start crying when Philomena Begley or Larry Cunningham came on the jukebox telling stories about orphans and teddy bears. Sometimes they even danced with each other and one would most definitely be prompted to consider: 'Perhaps there are more pussies who frequent this establishment than might at first appear!' Although it must be said and firmly insisted upon that tootles did not truly attend with interest of any depth until yum yum Mama songs they lit the night. 'One has hair of silvery grey, the other has hair of gold. One is my mother, God rest her, I love her, and the other is my sweetheart.' Tears down all those ruddy cheeks now coursing! 'I love my mammy!' Of course you do, my darling dear, but then do not we all? But we don't break up an entire café over it! As Donegal Danny did once. 'I'll break this fucking place in two! I'll bury it in rubble if you say that I don't love her! I loved her more that anyone that ever walked this earth! You hear me? You fucking hear me?'

And then in the plate of chips go sob sob sob. Poor Donegal Danny. Poor lonely man. His mama but bare bones upon the mountain!

As there I sat, the same thing thinking! But not to Mrs Begley listening! To Hawkwind and 'Silver Machine', the very same tears my own cheeks streaking as I thought of my old friends, on coffee-soaked paper scribbling letters: 'Write to me—this place is fucking crazy! Sometimes, I'm afraid, I don't feel so good! I love you Charlie, Irwin! And if not that, then once more thinking of her I'd give my life to find the one-and-only Eily Bergin. 'Where are you, Mammy?' I might often be heard to choke. 'Where are you?'

For how long already have one been searching? Since the every day of arrival, to be honest! Once—can you believe it!—a pallid face observing in a passing tube: 'It's her I swear it's her!', for Mitzi she did, in truth, resemble! Mitzi as she might be now in 1973! How many people in this teeming city? Ten million? More? How long to find one's mammy? Has anyone seen my mammy?

Look—there she is in the empty church. Turning her head to greet you.

'Hello, Paddy. Why did you leave it so long?'

As 'Ah' goes, thorned head upturned: 'Ah! Did you think it was your mammy?'

And in a café too, of course! From the street you saw her

75

and you passed, sitting there, pale hands curled around a cup.

'Mammy!'

'I beg your pardon?'

How many times did that one happen? Why, hundreds, dearest, hundreds!

Now is it any wonder that a bitterness would begin to grip, as through the small hours you sat there glass-eyed, gazing, while on the portable TV the Israeli tanks moved across the Sinai desert, their guns rat-tatting and repeating in your head.

Quite what I would have done without old Bertie Wooster and his baldy chap, I really do not know!

Chapter Twenty-One

Welcome Home!

It must straight away be acknowledged—for what is the point of deception—that poor old Bertie bore absolutely no resemblance to Marlon Brando (Some hope! Mr. Magoo might have been more like it!) who was up to his margarine tricks in France in the Odeon, Leicester Square, the billboard for which you could clearly see through the window of the cafe where Berts, man-about-town, was sitting now, daffoldil-coloured (the outfits!) in his lambswool V-neck and matching slacks, with the eminence P. Pussy, who thanks to a temporary change in her fortunes was looking, it had to be admitted, quite desirable, in her brightly-coloured suede patchwork jacket and a dinky little T-shirt with a scarlet baby heart over the left breast. Not to mention trousers most exceptionally delicious, of velvet once again and a big-buckled belt of patent black. With her eyeshadow laden and hair again dyed: boy with the swirling, shiny hair—could it be Pussy? Methinks it is!—did she perhaps resemble Miss Lynsey de Paul? She certainly did, let there be no doubt! Indeed often swinging her hips while working Piccadilly, to the tune of '*Sugar Me!*'—for services rendered, of course!

And now she sits there facing dearest Berts! Marlon Margarine definitely not—but everyone's favourite uncle perhaps. The one who always arrives with prezzies and is never done trying to amuse everyone—squirting you with his novelty trick flower and going: 'Ha ha! Only joking!', flopping down in his favourite armchair—the one he sits in every year—and ruffling the heads of kiddies all around as he says: 'Well! Wot's been 'appening then? Any stories for your Uncle Bertie?' As they all say: 'Oh! Uncle Berts! How we love him!'

Except when he gets too drunk of course, and starts blubbering in the corner and wilting like a great big daffodil (he just loved yellow!), saying nobody loved him and that his life had come to nothing. Uncle Bertie plastered across the table at every single wedding, everyone mortified with shame.

And now, here he was at it again in front of a complete stranger! Oh, Bertie Bertie Berts—what a sight to behold after practically a crate of beer! Holsten Pils like dribbly teeth going *plok*! as his spidery eyes they liquidized upon the table.

But waking up—eureka!—just as his favourite song came on the jukebox! How he adored them, Peters and Lee! As he did not fail to inform the entire company!

'I can't believe it! It's on! My favourite song! What a coincidence! Astonishing, in fact!'

It was unlikely, as a general rule, old Berts deciding at the drop of a hat to entertain crowed cares to renditions of '*Welcome Home*' or indeed any other popular numbers, but right at that very moment, at 3 A.M. on the 11th of August 1973, there would have been very little that anyone who took the notion could have done to stop him! He even insisted on his new companion—*moi*, of course!—accompanying him on a waltz around the floor, much to the amusement of the assorted Irish, Turkish and other immigrant workers who cried: 'Drop the hand!', 'Pair of Hoors!' and 'Get them off ya!'

As Berts crooned in Puss's tender ear: 'Welcome Home! Welcome! Come on in and close the door!'

Later—much later! (already the tubes were groaning into life), over a very appreciable number of Pils, it transpired that Berts had a theory. 'Gasp!', I counterfeited admirably. Yes, Berts went on, he had no doubt whatsoever that this particular song, as written, told only half the story.

I nodded feverishly as he stared into my eyes with something, if you didn't know better, you might be inclined to consider very close indeed to complete and utter madness, of a firmly pathological and obsessive kind, and not been in the slightest bit surprised if they had stormed the café and carted him off for good never to be seen again. Especially when he poked his finger into your chest and plaintively cried: 'What about the *inside* of the house? Eh? The *tables* and *chairs* and *sideboards* and that? You don't hear about them, do you? Oh no!' Out of nowhere he began to sing (And what a performer! I did you not!), twirling in and out among the tables.

Welcome Home Welcome
You've been gone too long

I nearly fell off the chair as stalk-eyed he leaned right in to me and continued:

Come on in you're home once more!

He slapped his perfectly manicured hand down on the formica.

'You've got to hear about the *inside*, don't you understand! And I'm going to see to it that we do! Oh, yes I've got my own band you know! Been in showbusiness all my life! I've written it already, actually! Yes! Welcome Home Part 2, I suppose you could call it. You want to hear it, my young friend?'

Before I could open my mouth, he beamed and drained his bottle, coughing politely as he began to sing to the waking city:

> Tables and chairs, pictures on the walls
> Come on in, right in through the hall!

It's hard to know what to say about him, old Berts, sitting there with his drinky and swaying from side to side, like a supperclub crooner lost in space.

'Every Sunday morning down the Wheatsheaf—it's how I earn my living! Just me and the jolly old keyboard, Patrick, my friend!'

Then Bertie—all of a sudden getting naughty! Almost breathless, as he squeezed my arm.

'Please! Please you'll come and stay with me!'

'Oh, I don't know about that now! A girl's got to think of her future, Bertie, darling!'

'I'll give you anything you want!'

'You will . . . ?

Naughty Pussy, gold-digging girl!

'Please say you will—Louise won't mind!'

'Louise!' I gasp. *'Louise?'*

'Yes! You can be my nephew!'

Much thought then given to it—approximately fifteen seconds worth that is! After all, I really did think I had had quite enough of Paddy Braden's High Class Escort Service, The Railings, Piccadilly Circus, London W1, for quite some time, thank you very much!

Some Information About Charlie and Irwin, Gleaned from Charlie's Letters

Charlie and Irwin walk down the street. Irwin is sullen with his hands in his pockets and from the petrol pumps to the chickenhouse not so much as a word passes between them.

'Don't lie to me!, says Charlie then. 'I'm not a fucking idiot! I don't believe your fucking stories!'

'I told you—I'm not going on any operations,' says Irwin.

'I sell *Republican News*—big deal!'

'You're a fucking liar and if you don't tell me the truth, I'll finish with you!'

Which she won't, of course, no matter what he says. But he *is* going on operations. In fact on the night before this conversation had helped two volunteers to prepare a booby-trap bomb.

'I don't care what you believe!' cried Charlie. 'It's not in you to kill someone!'

'What do you know? What the fuck do you know, Charlie?'

A lot more—certainly about 'Volunteer' Irwin Kerr than he would—or could—care to admit!

As was plainly evident only some nights later (not long after the young McCarville fellow came sailing down the river roped to a mattress with a six-inch nail hammered into his head and it had been decided something needed to be done) when the Horse Kinnane and Jackie Timlin called for him and they drove off to stiff old Anderson and his son. Who both conveniently happened to be in the library spraying food onto some exotic plant or other when the three masked desperadoes bust in. Nutting the old chap proved no problem but his son (albeit he was fifty years of age) fought tooth and nail. Almost escaped, indeed, before the Horse managed to get between him and the door, knocking him to his knees and shouting: 'Do him! Do him!, Kerr, you bollocks you!'

As Irwin stood there pissing himself—he really did, as anyone with an eye in their head could see from the gathering map on the crotch of his trousers, and being so far away in some other place that eventually Jackie had to push him out of the way, snatch the gun from his hand and put three in your man's head. 'You stupid fucker, Kerr! You stupid dithering little fuck! What do you think this is? What do you think it is?'

Irwin wasn't quite sure what it was. All he knew was that from that night on, things were never going to be quite the same again. As indeed they weren't. It didn't take the cops long to figure out who was involved and after that any time Irwin crossed the border, they pulled him in. At first he was just as tough and resilient as you could get. But that didn't last long. And when they said that they were going to see that Charlie was set up and busted for dope, then things began to take a different turn. Especially when they did stop her and mysteriously find a tiny bit of grass in her pocket. It was nothing but when word got out, her old pair were mortified. 'Next time,' the cops said, 'she's fucked, Kerr. Unless you start seeing some sense.'

He knew enough to know that if he started seeing some

sense *he* was fucked. But which he did—partly because he wasn't sleeping anymore and couldn't think straight. Half the time he didn't even know what he was doing. Clearly it was only a matter of time before he started singing like a canary. 'I can't lose Charlie,' he kept repeating to himself, 'If anything happened to her. . . .'

Which, fortunately, because of his ultimately tragic co-operation nothing did, apart from the fact that she looked like having a fantastic career in the National College of Art and Design.

Chapter Twenty-Two

At Last I Get to Paint Them!

About which she told me everything the day I rang her!

'At last, Patrick! At last I get to paint the fuckers! Two thousand dead ones on a big black background!'

'I got you the Yes albums,' I told her. 'They're on the way.'

'You fucking beauty,' she said. 'How are they treating you over there? Things any better yet?'

'They have the arse rode off me,' I said.

'You fucking slut,' she said and down the mouthpiece blew a kiss.

'Good luck,' I said and by the surging throng once more was swallowed up.

Chapter Twenty-Three

Up West!

It's Sa'day night dahn the old West End, innit? Fackin' right it is, mah san! Look at 'em puntahs—'avin 'emselves a right old time, they are! And wot's wrong wiv that, ai? Naffink! Not a bleedin' 'fing, mate! Ain't like they ain't worked bleedin' 'ard for it all week, geddin' themselves lookin' narce nah for a night aht on the old tahn. Look at them in there—laverly, I tell yah!—fackin' laverly!—quaffin' the old vino and whackin' 'em all dahn, them great big steaks! Bless 'em, that's wot I say. Every last soddin, one of 'em! Like bleedin' Christmas it is in there, watchin 'em 'frow it back, larfing their bleedin' 'eads off at some soddin' stupid joke! But who cares—a larf's a larf, innit? I don't give a fack, I really don't, wot people larfs abaht—long as they's 'avin themselves a good time, that's awright by me! All them lights—running along the edge of the window—looks so soddin' invitin', you know? Like—no need to stay aaht there—come right on in, guv'—come and join the party!

BANG!

Now wot the bleedin' 'ell was that? Oh, for cryin' aht lahd! Look at that! Poor geezer's got blood runnin' all down side of 'is face! It's a diabolical liberty, that is! 'Frowing bombs into restaurants! Wot do they 'ope to gain by that—ai? Bladdy 'ell! They're all cammin' aht nah—screamin' and crying some of 'em, it's like somefink you'd se in a bleedin' 'orror movie! Poor bloke didn't even get the steak far as 'is marf, blew his fackin' 'ead off! Oh, nao! Look at that little old lady! Where's 'er legs then? Gao on—tell me! Where's the old gel's legs? That's right—she ain't got none, 'as she? Blown raht dahn to stumps, they are—all because of them bleedin' Paddies! Cor, it don't arf try your patience, I'll tell you! Take 'em over 'ere, give 'em jobs and wot do they do? Blow your fackin' head off! Weren't to be seen doing much av it during the last war though, if you recall! Blahdy bog Arabs! I'm sorry, guv, but that's the way I feel! Wot if it 'ad been my old mum in there—or yours? Send 'em all back, that wot I say. Back to the bleedin' bog wot shat 'em aht in the first place!

Chapter Twenty-Four

A Big Dead Flower

An attitude certainly not held by good old Bertie and that pinky perky baldy lad of his—he just couldn't get enough of Paddies and Pussies! Had gone stark raving bonkers over me ever since I talked him into letting me sing a song or two down the Wheatsheaf every Sunday morning. My training with Charlie back in the good old days of the Juke Box Jury Shows was certainly beginning to pay off now! Did I mention earlier that I am the proud possessor of quite an excellent singing voice? Well—let me take this opportunity to announce it now! Not that it should come as any surprise when one considers that dear old Pop was renowned the length and breadth of the country for his beautiful tenor renditions at weddings and similar public gatherings of such classics as 'Goodbye' from *The White Horse Inn*, 'Blaze Away', and, surprisingly perhaps, '*Paddy McGinty's Goat*'. Not, mind you, that I had any intentions of carrying on the family tradition! At least not in quite the same manner as dear old Dad, as the Wheatsheaf clientele discovered that first Sunday morning when Bertie adjusted his cravat (yellow too—with little back spots!), hit a few chords on the Hammond and declared: 'Ladies and gentlemen! This morning I have a very special guest! All the way from the Emerald Isle—it's Miss Dusty Springfield!'

As out I wiggled—truly over the top, I swear!—and launched into the most fabulous version ever of '*The Windmills of Your Mind*', completely losing myself in it when I got to the bit about the world being just an apple whirling silence in space. I don't think I was in the hotel at all for three whole minutes, Dusty waltzing through the vast and shining firmament with a microphone in her hand. After that, for mischief, I belted out: '*Son of a Preacher Man*' and have to say I brought the house down! I thought Bertie was going to explode with sheer unadulterated pride! Every time I looked over (I don't know how many curtain calls I took!) there he was clapping away like a little boy who wants to tell everyone: 'I know her! She's my friend!'

Well, did I get on like a house on fire in that old Whatsheaf! It simply became the highlight of my week, and for days before it I'd get myself into a right old tizzy trying to decide both what to wear and what I was going to sing. (Wardrobe—including beehive Dusky wig—funded by Berts, of course!) Sometimes I could get into such a state about it, I'd take the head off poor Berts—'Why can't you help me! Why!'—but when I'd calmed down we always made it up—those sad dog eyes of his always won me over anyway. Mostly I did the Supremes, Dusty and, of course, Lulu. I used to go crazing doing her number 'Shout!'—standing upon on the tables and everything. And being a right old tart raising my sequinned mini to drive them mad!

After each gig then, we'd drink ourselves silly, me and Berts, and then when we got home, it would be out with the baldy lad and poor old Daffodil Man losing his marbles again. 'Oh, how I love you!' he'd groan, and what could I do but laugh when I'd look at him standing there with his stalk saluting and the canary-coloured trousers like an accordion around his ankles! 'Uh! Uh! *Uh*!' Was all you could hear then as you held a big dead flower in your arms.

Chapter Twenty-Five

A Little Curling Whisper: Why?

Yes, good old Berts and me—just two people who wanted to be with one another, to live together, as the New Seekers would have it, 'in perfect harmony', unlike Louise our darling landlady whose scorching glares of late we'd had to endure, and who now missed no opportunity whatsoever to bark: 'Shut that door behind you!', flicking tea towels for all she was worth as she demanded to know: 'Who left those cups there—they're filthy!', in between lapsing into semitrances as she remembered once again her poor son Shaunie run over by a bus in 1961. 'She never got over it, you know,' Berts told me. 'Police arrived at the door one day—and that was it, really.'

I felt sorry for Louise. I knew how she felt. With her it was her son, with me a mother—it was the same thing all in all. Which maybe explains why I fell for her and she for me! And did it drive old Bertie Mad!

How it happened was just as simple as it was unexpected, I have to say. Sitting there on the sofa minding my own business one day, sipping a lemonade and watching *The Wombles*, of all things, when next thing you know I hear this sniffling noise and she's beside me with a Kleenex and going into the whole story about her husband leaving and how she had loved him, her darling Ginger, anything she would have done for him, she said, why did he leave me, why? She asked me, then before I could answer, putting her arm around my neck and kissing me so hard I thought I'd choke. But I wasn't complaining, mind! Even when I fell on the floor and banged my head and she kept gasping: 'Darling! Oh, my fucking darling! Ginger!'

Which is hilarious really, because to tell you the truth, I'm sure she was only putting that on and had wanted to call me Shaunie all along!

Probably if I hadn't been used to dressing up as a matter of course, I wouldn't have agreed her scheme (which started when we were pie-eyed one night) with the shorts and the Shaunie suit and everything. Believe it or not, I was even a little bit embarrassed the first time we did it, and I'd had at least four gins too! But after a while I got more than accustomed to the little grey jacket and the short trousers and really began to get excited when she asked me to call her 'Mammy' which, apparently, because of his dad being Irish, was exactly the way Shaunie pronounced it. 'O my silly boy, my Shaunies!' she'd say, and I'd say: 'Mammy!' After a while I started to really like it, just sitting there on her knee and being engulfed by all this powdery warm flesh. I never wanted to get up in fact.

Until, one day, quite unexpectedly, who happens along only Berts! There is no point in pretending I was anything other than embarrassed out of my life when he snapped: 'What the bloody hell is going on here!' in this shaky voice, because I hadn't said anything to him about what was going on—as well as being in the middle of sucking her nipple and going: 'Mammy!'

Well you can imagine, all hell broke loose after that! Lucky for Louise, Bertie had never been much of a fighter, flapping away like a demented seagull in between protests of: 'It's not fair!' and 'He's my girlfriend, you fucking old cow! Mine!'

We were all in a right old state after that incident, I'm afraid. All I can remember is poor old Bertie coming up the stairs, whimpering: 'He's not a schoolboy! He's my girl and you have no right to be doing this to him!'

It was a hard decision for me to have to make but I'm afraid that Louise as part of the bargain had been doing my hair so beautifully—with pins and clips and slides, not to mention providing me with creams and lotions for your skin that you would absolutely die for, that in the end I had no choice but to say to him: 'Sorry, Bertie. I really am so sorry.'

He was heartbroken and left that very night. I never saw him again. Then it was straight into Louise's arms to hug her again and hug her and hug her.

The only thing about it being that somewhere at the back of my mind, I kept thinking: 'You shouldn't be doing this, as you well know. She's not your mammy. If she wants you to be her son, that's fine. But she's not your mammy. Your mammy was special. Even if she did dump you on Whiskers Braden's step and leave you for ever. Even if she did do that, no one—no one!—could ever take her place. So why are you sitting on a strange woman's knee, Patrick Braden?'

I'd try my best not to let it come and would furiously suck on the nipple, but somehow it always did, a little curling whisper: '*Why?*'

Chapter Twenty-Six

'My Name's Not Eily Bergin!'

Some days when she'd gone shopping, I'd go out and walk the streets alone, just to get as far away as I could from the house. It must have been around that time it started, for any time I saw a woman standing at a bus stop or whatever, I wouldn't be able to help myself and the next thing you'd know, some complete stranger would be standing back going: 'What are you on about? My name's not Bergin! Nor Eily neither! Get lost before I call the police!'

I made more mistakes like that—but there's no point in me pretending! I just couldn't help myself!

If Terence Were to See Me Now!

Moping about in my silly old housecoat—actually I don't think he'd be all that surprised, to be honest with you! 'I think the truth, Patrick,' I can hear him saying, 'is that maybe you always secretly wanted to *become* her, Eily. After all—she could hardly walk away then!'

You have to hand it to Terence, even if he did leave! He was the only one in the hospital who knew anything. Some of the idiots they brought about the place! Fenshaw! I mean, for God's sake! 'Oh, it's perfectly clear that your provincial small-town Irish background has left you ill-equipped to deal with the challenges of a major cosmopolitan city!' Oh, well, excuse me, Dr Essence Of Insight, how extraordinarily perceptive!

Was it any wonder I fed him al load of lies about feeling oppressed and being a key figure along in the IRA English bombing campaign! Which he swallowed, of course—hook, line and sinker!—the great old idiot!

Catch my real doctor falling for that. I loved Terence so much. I even used to dream about him. I felt so secure with him around. I suppose I ought to have known that one day they'd come along and say: 'Oh, Doctor Harkin? He's leaving. Doctor Fenshaw will be taking over from now on!'

I'm afraid the truth is you're putting yourself in for plenty of disappointment if you expect people to hang around for very long in this life!

After they told me he was gone for good, I kept hoping that against all the odds he'd return. When I had the argument with Fenshaw, they brought a Dr Murti who said he wanted to be my friend but most of the time I didn't know he was there. Instead of talking, I'd just sit there and do what Terence had told me to—write it out so I could somehow make sense of it all. I wonder what he'd have made of the hundreds of pieces I wrote about him, fibbing old Gregory Peck!

I don't know how many times I've read this following bit, it makes me feel so warm and cosy!

Chapter Twenty-Seven

Terence in a Sheepskin

It was Christmas and I couldn't believe my eyes when I saw Terence. What was the best of all was that his stupid old doctor's coat was gone and he was wearing this lovely fur-lined sheepskin jacket and a big red woolly scarf. He looked so Christmassy! 'Patrick!' he said and gave me a smile. 'Bet you didn't think I'd come back, did you?' 'Oh, Terence!' I cried, and ran to him. I just couldn't keep my hands off him. He told me how much he missed me. 'I'd never have gone if it could have been avoided,' he said. 'You do understand that, don't you?' I stroked his cheek and said: 'You know I do! Mr. Bushy-Eyes!' Then we kissed and I made us some lovely hot cocoa which we had with plum pudding. How long did he stay with me? One whole week, actually! You don't believe me? Well, I'm sorry about that! Because I don't care, you see! Believe what you like! The fact is he stayed for one whole week and we loved one another like any man and woman should. I lay there in his arms and Perry Como sang: 'Have Yourself a Merry Little Christmas'. It was so funny because I had to strip a silver tinsel around my neck like a necklace and Terence kept calling me 'His Christmas Angel'. We both agreed that Christmas-time was our

97

favourite time of the year. 'For as long as I live, I want to spend it with you,' I said and he said: 'My darling.' I don't know whether it was the mulled wine or that silly song '*On The Trail Of The Lonesome Pine*!' by Laurel and Hardy that he put on or a combination of both but by the end of the evening I was in fits, I really was, and every time they'd go: '*On The Trail Of The Lonesome Pine*!', I would erupt again. 'Patrick!' Terence would say. 'What on earth is wrong with you?' and I'd choke: 'O Terence! Terence! Terence!'

It wasn't the mulled wine at all, of course, as silly me realized later—it was the music, reminding me as it did of all those wonderful, happy Christmasses we'd had down the years at home in Rat Trap Mansions ('God I love them,' Mammy Whiskers would say—O but of course she would!— 'Good old Stan Laurel and Oliver Hardy! This is another fine mess youse have got me into! God but aren't they great, my happy, special, loving and adoring family!')

Chapter Twenty-Eight

Dancing on a Saturday Night

And then you'd think: 'What a wonderful place it truly is, this world in which we wander!' As you casually pick up the newspaper and, surprise, once more it is a balmy night in little Belfast town. Which is why the soldiers are aht and abaht, having themselves a good old piss-up like! All red-cheeked and rosy as out of the barracks they go and down the street they ramble, not giving a toss about the 'facking war!', as one of them says while he lights a fag. 'It's the politicians wot facks it ap! Let 'em go and fack 'emselves!' Which is what they fully intend to do this Friday night, shirts wide-open to the waist, as into the disco bar they troop. Three pints of Harp and the ultra-violet strobes lighting up them sweet and fancy girls—especially two sitting over in the corner. Who are giving the soldiers the gamey eye—and does it take them long to spot it? No, sir! And before you know it, are over in a flash, pulling up chairs and rubbing hands and asking them how they're feeling girls!

'Och we're awright, lek! And how are youse?'

'Feelin' pretty good nah, I don't mind tellin' you! Right, lads?'

To which the response it sure is: 'Yes!'

The girls they truly look fantastic—done up to the nines in their turtlenecks and wet-look minis, the make-up laid on with a trowel. And the smell of perfume? Phew! And watch them dance now on that floor, despite the high cork wedgies!

'So—what sort of music you like then, girls?'

'We like Barry Blue!' they cry and do the shaky-shakies for all they are worth!

As Barry belts it out across the town!

> Pretty little girl with your dancing shoes
> A gold satin jacket and a silvery blouse
> And it'll be all right
> Dancing on a Saturday night!

> Well the jukebox is playin' like a one-man band
> It's the only kinda music, girl, we both
>   understand
> And it'll be all right
> Dancin' on a Saturday night!

Well, what a time they are having! How many vodkas did everyone have? No one could remember! All anyone could remember was the girls puckering up their noses and going:

'Youse boys! Youse are wild cheeky so youse are! But we like youse anyway! Fancy a wee drink somewhere else maybe?'

'Sounds good to me, lads—ai? But where are we gonna get a drink in Belfast at this hour of the night?'

'Well—it just happens there's this wee party, see! Right, Deirdre?'

'Wee bit of a shingdig!'

'What are we waiting for then! Let's go!'

*

The sitting room they arrive at—it's beautifully kept—there's no doubt about it. Nice polished sideboards and in the corner—a fabulous mahogany piano.

'Just the spot for a party!' say the lads, shouldering the six-packs.

'And look! More drink!' they shout, throwing open a cupboard and taking out a bottle of vodka to crack open with the girls, except that when they look the girls aren't there anymore. Instead there are four men who knew the job would be so easy they didn't bother putting masks on. In literally a matter of seconds the sitting room is just about the last place on earth you would want to hold a party. In one of the soldier's heads there was a faint echo of Barry Blue singing.

'Fucking scum,' the men say as they stop the Cortina to dump them on the waste ground and go off to a club for a drink.

Thinking Far Too Much

That was what Terrence said. That I was thinking far too much about everything and I know he was right of course but what could I say? I could hardly say: 'You can't waste life, Terence! Life is precious! If it's given, you must treasure and protect it! Not throw it away, turn your back on it and cast it aside!'

Because then he would have thought I was feeling sorry for myself and bringing it all back to that morning on Whisker's step. But I wasn't—I just genuinely felt that if you could bring someone into this world then it is your responsibility to care for and look after them! And if you don't, then you are wrong and I don't care who you are!

I was sorry for upsetting Terence that day I started crying and saying that Mammy was wrong for leaving me and not coming back! I wasn't blaming her for leaving but she should have come back! She should have come back or wrote to me or something! She should never have just gone like that! For without her, how can I ever belong on this earth?

And that is exactly, exactly, what it would have been like for Martina Sheridan's baby if she had one! Which was all I was trying to say to her. I just wanted her to see sense, that was all—because I knew that no one else would!

For the simple reason that they don't understand! No one else understands! They just don't understand!

Understand

The Martina episode—or, I suppose what you could call: '*The Incident behind the Creamery*', took place much later—in early 1975, about two months after I arrived back from England. I know I hadn't been feeling well but you couldn't have described me as '*mad*' or anything like that. Terence said that all that was wrong with me was that I was hypersensitive to the things that were going on around me and I think he was right. Perhaps in retrospect it was heedless of me to wear a dress or any other kind of clothes like that, but I was so worried about Charlie and other things that it just never occurred to me. I mean, it wasn't as if I was swanning about the village like a tart or something—it just wasn't like that! I had far too much on my mind, for Charlie was in an absolutely awful state because of Irwin's death, she really was. Had gone completely haywire and been thrown out of the art college, in fact, drinking her head off from morning till night, her skill all blotchy from the vodka, and her clothes—before we moved in together (I started washing them after that)—actually beginning to smell. So it really was appalling, I'm not exaggerating. Close to unbearable, in fact, until she began to slowly calm, sleep coming back to her at nights.

What had happened with Irwin, I forgot to describe, was that everybody decided he had given enough information—'sung enough' as they said—and Jackie and the

Horse Kinnane took him out to the bog to kill him. I think it was when Charlie saw him in the shabby old overalls (his pathetic death-suit) with a bit of refuse bag hood still stuck to his collar that she decided she couldn't be bothered pretending any more. She just went.

Perhaps, with hindsight, I did behave rashly. But all I wanted to do was explain to Martina. I just wanted her to understand.

Chapter Twenty-Nine

The Incident Behind the Creamery

A lot of people said that I slapped her across the face—I did not! I said: 'Look, Martina! All I want to do is talk to you! If you will only listen to me—all it will take is five minutes, I promise you!' I know I ought to have had the sense not to ask her that. But now that I'd gone so far, there wasn't an awful lot I could do. All I remember is taking her by the arms and saying: 'Martina! There are things you should know about. These people are just using you! You're only fifteen! Do you think any of them will care if you bring an unwanted child into the world? You know what they want, don't you? Don't you? You know all they want!' I think what probably upset me more than anything was her shouting out Smigs' name. All I could hear was 'Smigs! Smigs!' and that was why I shook her. I mean—you have no idea what he was like! Once—not long after I came back to Tyreelin—I was standing in the shop queue and he lifted up my dress with a bicycle pump. I was sure it was all a joke you see and that the people were well-used to me by now. (I was wrong, of course—I can see that now. The only reason the 'Hello, honky tonks and 'Ooh, you are awfuls' had stopped was that they wanted absolutely *nothing* to do with me.) Which I hope explains why I turned around and smiled at him. It was just a big, completely unoffended smile but when I saw the expression on his face, it frightened me, it really and truly did. All I can say is that the eyes seemed dead—frighteningly dead in his head. All I wanted to do then was just run out of the shop and stay locked in the house for days. Not even tell Charlie about it. Just lock myself in my room and try not to think of it, hoping it would go away, the thought of his face. So you can imagine how I felt now when straight away Martina started it again. 'Smigs! Smigs!' was all you could hear. I don't care what lies she told around the village—I didn't slap her. It was just a sharp, firm tap, that's all, solely to calm her down.

I had heard them saying that Smigs had been in a fight in the Sports Centre and had opened some person's face with a straight razor. That was what kept going through my mind and we stood there behind the creamery, both white, facing one another.

'Please listen to me, Martina! Stay away from Tommy McNamee! List to me, please!' I pleaded, but she wouldn't. 'Let me go,' she said, 'you get your hands off me now and let me go, you fucking queer!'

All that I could get to come into my head then was the thought of Tommy McNamee (her 'boyfriend'—he was twenty years married, for God's sake!) slowly pulling his jeans down and whispering into her ear: 'You're the nicest girl in the village, Martina. That lovely wavy blonde hair of yours is enough to turn any man's head!' and her cheeks flushing scarlet with all his flattery—because, of course, she didn't know any better. How could she? How was she to know that all he cared about was pleasuring himself and walking away then to boast about it?

While she would be left there—abandoned—for what other word is there for it?—worrying herself sick whether or not she was going to miss her period. And then, worst of all, discovering that, already growing inside her, that was a tiny little baby—the father of whom she would probably never know. On one particular evening, after seeing McNamee leaving his house to go to meet her, it had been all I could do to run out and cry: 'Leave her alone! Why can't you leave her alone!' heartbroken by the thought of that innocent, credulous face.

I knew for a long time the covetous way he and others had been looking at her. Once, when I went into Mulvey's for change, I saw her leaning across the pool table and one of them publicly feeling himself. She didn't know this, of course, just like so many young girls of her age don't. Can't possibly, I suppose. Until it is too late. The estate in Tyreelin is full of them. Barely over fourteen, some of them, already pushing buggies and looking years older than they are. And their children. Who can say it's fair the way some of them are treated? You can tell by their complexions—the pasty, porridgy skin colour that they all seem to have, left outside bars with mucus on their noses, chewing at their fingers and staring with those sad old, empty eyes. Eyes that say: '*Who will love me? Why will no one love me?*' And not with the sort of emotion that Martina Sheridan had been duped into accepting as genuine. A few groping stokes and a stab between the legs behind the dilapidated creamery! That wasn't what they meant and it wasn't how it was supposed to be! Life is pure! Precious! To be treasured! Why couldn't Sheridan see that? 'Why can't you listen, Martina!' I cried. 'If not for your own, then for your baby's sake!'

There was so much going through my head that although we had only been standing by the shed for over a minute or so, to me it seemed like eons. I had managed—I know now it was silly—to get myself into quite a state and if I did shake her again or call her names—I'm sorry, I truly am.

Another thing I will admit to that was silly and I don't even know what made me to it—I asked Terence but he wasn't sure either—('Perhaps seeking the source of life?' he said. 'To protect it, do you think?')—was going down to the creamery after dark and crawling around on my hands and knees with a flashlight, looking for traces of semen. I suppose I thought that if I didn't find any, I could feel relieved that perhaps he had used a condom and that, if I did, I would feel, perversely, somewhat better because at least I knew the truth. Why I broke down after putting my hand directly on some that had spilled on a dockleaf I'm not really sure—I think it was because it seemed so ridiculous that such a minuscule amount of liquid could cause so much heartache. But which it did, as I'd always known, and consequently belonged in a world thousands of miles from the one I'd written of and dreamed for Terence. Of which he spoke so highly, saying that never before had he read anything like it.

*

Was I *chuffed* when he said that? How much I cannot tell you, because it meant so much to me too. Do you know what he *actually* said?

He said it was beautiful, my little piece about home.

Chapter Thirty

Chez Nous

It was a nice, quiet evening in the townland of Tyreelin. Up above in the sky, the stars are out and in each and every house that dots the village square, there are little rectangles of amber and from the chimneys, tiny curls of smoke both blue and grey. Here in this one small cottage, there is a feeling of peacefulness. Which is so overwhelming that it appears as if this is how it has been right from the beginning of time. What we see before us is a fine, stone cottage, built by the labouring hands of a gentle, strong man who is husband to the woman who now softly reads to her bright baby boy whose name is known to all as Patrick. Is this Patrick— Pat Puss of the girly doodle dandies, son-of-priest and naughty nipple-licker of a Mum called Louise Ward—fame? No—this is simple, ordinary Patrick—son of the man called Daddy, who with great big shovel hands this cabin proudly raised. Sweet Eily who perhaps once made breakfast for a lascivious, hungry cleric?

But no, my friends. Eily it may be, but not that one. This is Eily Mammy, indeed one of the most beautiful that ever was. Who, with her magic, sweetens every page she turns. 'Listen to me now,' she whispers, 'as I speak of a little fellow who went to travel, walked the world, up hill and down dale, but always with his mammy by his side.' Are Patrick's eyes star-bright? And do his thoughts they not run thus?: 'This is my mother. She is the most beautiful that ever was and I would die if anything happened to her.'

But, of course, nothing will happen to her! Look at her now as she approaches the oven of the blackleaded range, her hands covered with a bluecheck cloth, out to whip a tray of steaming apple cakes! 'Hooray!' cries Patrick. 'Apple cakes! My favourite!'

As in comes Daddy, hardy brow sweatbeaded as he licks his lips and, with a flick of his black-haired, handsome head, declares: 'H'ho! What's this! Well, whatever it is—it's smelling good!'

And then to the table all—Daddy, Patrick and Eily, wonder-mother of the world.

—Do you love your mammy? says Daddy then and smiles.
—I love her millions, Dad, his son replies.
—And why is that, now tell us!
—Because she's my mam!
—Because she's your mammy!
—Who bakes bread.
—Bread!
—And buns!
—And scrubs the floor!
—And loves her little Patrick!
—The finest mam in the whole wide world!

And now, at last, small Patrick sleeps. The soundest

sleep of any toddler since this world of ours began. In the corner—the shadowy figure of a parish priest with his soutane raised and his great big angry tootle glaring out? Of course not, sillies!

The silhouette of a silky man with a silk garrotte who smiles to the strains of a summer song as your last ebb of life chokes out? For heaven's sake!

No, nothing only silence, and upon the walls a picture with the words *Chez Nous*, embroidered with blue entwining flowers. *This is our little home.* As family now it snoozes and over the night sky closes.

And Patrick in his dreams, he thinks: 'I am so happy, and I thank God for giving me this, but most especially for my mammy.'

Chapter Thirty-One

Running Out on Louise

Why I had to go and do a stupid thing like blab it all to Louise instead of keeping it to myself like the most private, intimate secret that it was is still beyond me for she didn't have to know it, it wasn't going to make the slightest difference to her, for up until then we'd been having the most fantastic time, we really had and if you'd said to me that I was going to turn against her, never mid run out of the house shaking and shouting, absolutely high as a kite, I simply wouldn't have been able to believe you.

Not that we weren't capable of such high jinks in other ways, not half we weren't, her coming in with that look in her eye and then crooking her finger until off I'd go like a lamb, up on her knee then in shorts with her going: 'Mr. Wonderful' and the glimmer of a tear in her eye as she ran her fingers through my hair. That, of course, was when it happened—me letting it all slip, I mean. Allowing myself to get carried away as I thought of Eily in that dancehall long ago, the way Benny Lendrum had told me she'd been, with her gorgeous bubble-cut hair, check blouse in yellow and capri pants in white, not a fellow in the place able to take his eyes off her. 'The most beautiful girl in the town,' Benny said. 'The one and only Eily Bergin—give your woman out of *South Pacific* a run for her money any day, they used to say!'

Which had really excited me when he said it for no one could say: 'Oh, that's just Braden again—making up stupid fantasies about his mother just because she was rode by a priest and then dumped him on a step in a bloody Rinso box!' That was one thing they couldn't say for as I sat there on the summer seat on that day in 1965, I had heard the words fall right from Benny's lips, one by one watching them fall and sparkle like gold.

*

'Oh, Louise!' I cried and threw my arms around her neck (delirious, which was how I let it slip). 'How beautiful she was I just cannot begin to tell you!' as she said: 'Hush!' and stroked my neck—making me go on and on, of course! And tell her everything—everything!

*

'Why did I have to say it, Terence! Why did I have to say it!' I begged him to tell me over and over. But Terence just nodded and said: 'Keep going.'

What I wanted him to understand was that I did love Louise, not in a pure way maybe, but in one that was sort of special because she had been so good to me and me being Shaunie of course had made me close as well (not to mention all the outfits she ran up for me—Audrey Hepburn, Dusty, Diana Ross—there isn't even any point in going into the work she put into those!)—but what she didn't understand, why couldn't she understand?, was that there are cer-

113

tain things you do not do, should not do—even begin to think of doing them. How could she not see that this was different to Shaunie and Dusty and everything else we'd done and that what I'd told her was mine and never meant to leave my lips. Why could she not see that, Terence?, I said. It was after I'd begun to explain all that to him he asked me was that the first time you felt whatever it is that holds you to the ground beginning to slip away? And I said yes it was, even though I'd felt the same after Silky—but had forgotten all about it for up until then I felt solid as a rock. Which is something I'd always wanted. To be able to say: '*This* is where I belong—right here in *this* place, blasted by wind and weather and never to be moved.' Instead of the very opposite which was about to happen now.

*

When she came into the room first, I didn't believe it was her. I felt my legs turning to string again and I moved back against the wall in case I'd collapse. Then my face flushed scarlet and I could feel the saliva in my mouth thickening up into something like jam. 'Like me?' she said, and began walking across the floor shaking invisible maraccas and batting her lashes the way she did. All of a sudden it was as if I hadn't washed in weeks as I thought: 'Why did I tell her about Mammy? Why did I have to *tell* her?'

Whiskers used to have this habit of lighting cigarette papers and sending them flying up the flue to the light, to go spinning across the stars as far as Pluto or wherever else they wanted to go and that was what I felt like now as I watched the blur of yellow that was the check shirt and the beautifully starched white Capri pants as she ran her hands over them singing: '*I'm gonna wash that man right outa my hair! I'm gonna wash that man right outa my hair!*'

I might have been a ball of fluff blown harum-scarum by her breath as she moved in close still singing it, but would never have floated quite so far if she hadn't uttered the words that left her lips then when I said: 'What are you doing? Louise, please—what are you doing?' as she raked her fingers through her bubble curls and tossing her head back, cried: 'At last I've come for him—my little Rinso baby!'

Terence told me it all dated back to then. 'You've never been quite with us since, have you?' and in a way I have to agree. I tried to explain to him what it was like when me and Charlie waltzed like we were two tiny birthday cake figures out in cosmos, way out among the distant planets, '*watching the earth down below,*' except with the one difference that it had been so beautiful—like it all belonged to you.

And now, here you were, rudderless, out there, not knowing where your arms or legs began, as you floated in a cosmos with no end.

'Why else did you run out that night?' Terence asked me. 'Was there something else she said?'

That was why I was so heartbroken when Terence left without telling me. Because he knew my story inside out and understood why I broke down. As he did now. 'Yes!' I spluttered through the tears. 'She said "Breakfast." She said: "Please stay for breakfast" or something stupid like that!'

I could see him looking at me so tenderly for a long time after that, then looking down at his notepad as he said softly: 'You hate that word, don't you?'

And I nodded. As he moved closer to me and put his strong hand in mine. Some people might think—like with Brendan Cleeve later on—that I am sort of a sex maniac because I say things like that. Sex was the furthest thing from my mind when I thought of it, his hand being strong. It was like it was gripping me and saying: 'You're down here now—rock solid! And this where you are going to be strong! For this is where you're going to stay from now on, Patrick! And that's the way it's going to be!'

It was as if I was looking though a skylight and out there in the stretched blackness there were thousands and thousands of weightless cigarette papers all going hither and thither except with one big difference this time—I wasn't one of them!

It was the most fantastic feeling I ever remember! Made even better by the fact that now Terence had his arm around me. Big oaken-armed Terence! Whose brown eyes twinkled as he said: 'I want to hear about him, the man who gave you life! The bastard you hate who dumped you on the step or started proceedings that led to it! We've got to hear, you hear me? We've got to hear—so get out there—write write write and fucking write!'

Can you imagine another doctor swearing? But that was Terence! He gripped me in them oaken arms and fixed me with those twinkly eyes: 'Will you?' he said. 'Will you?'

I thought I was skyward again!

'Yes I cried. 'Yes! Yes! Yes!' and nearly knocked him down in the rush to pen yet another of my famous masterpieces!

Chapter Thirty-Two

Visitations in the Night

by P. Braden, Ward 7

How difficult it is for the young seminarian getting to sleep at night! Particularly if you have been out on the playing field most of the day doing endless laps in the churning mud, not to mention God knows how many press-ups with Father Joe McGeaney shouting from the sideline like a madman: 'Ah, will you for the love of God put your backs into it! How in heaven's name do ye expect to face St Malachy's Magherafelt if that's the best performance ye can come up with! It's like watching a pack of old women! Football! That's not football! I could go down to Junior 1B right this very minute and pack a pair of young scabs that'd acquit themsleves better than that! McAlinden! What do you call that! You call that a free kick? Fit you better you'd pack your bags this very minute and clear off home to your father on the farm, for mucking out the byres is all you'll ever be any good for, as far as I can see!' After which the team trainer would gather a ball of phlegm in his throat, roll it around in the nether regions of his tonsils for some seconds, then propel it with great force so that it spun in the air before landing randomly on either a hoof-hole or tuft of grass directly in front of him, as he allowed himself a little smile, moving forward with his fingers interlaced beneath his back soutane, his priestly duck-like bottom obtruding. Because he was joking, of course. Well, not exactly joking perhaps, but when he said that McAlinden was of little use for anything but cleaning out the abodes of animals—that most certainly he did not mean. For, as he well knew, Pat Joe McAlinden was, if not the best and most consistent performer on the school team, certainly one he could least afford to do without. From the very start of the season, he had been an inspiration to the rest of the players. The man who had, almost single-handedly, been responsible for their passage into the semi-finals of the Leinster Cup. Which, of course, was to be played this very Saturday! Was it any wonder they were nervous? The miracle was that Father Joe didn't shout louder at his star player! After all—you had to make sure they didn't become too complacent, didn't you? He had been training the seminary football team long enough to know the pitfalls young men like McAlinden could stumble into. It wouldn't be the first time he'd seen young proteges of his undermine their brilliance through arrogance—refusing to pass the ball, attempting lyrical, complicated moves when all that was required was affirmative, unequivocal action. He wasn't about to let that happen, and if being hard on the boy was what was required, then so be it. And thus far, his tactics had worked like a dream for McAlinden. As Father Joe passed the goalposts and shaded his eyes from the flashing sun to determine the position of the ball, he considered that if that student continued the way he was going, he might well yet be in line for a senior prefectship. As the thought entered his mind, a little ripple of pride ran through the clergyman, for in fact it was fair to say that such an achievement, were it to become a reality, would be due in no small measure to the firmness and far-sightedness of his tutelage. O, good man Donegan! Did you see that one? A high, lobbying ball that almost slipped out of the goalkeeper's hands! What if they pulled off one like that on Saturday! It would be good to see the face of Father Jack McManus then! Father Jack was the trainer of St Malachy's, or St Mal's as they were known more or less for the duration of the competition. He'd have to shake Father Joe's hand when it was all over but it would still kill him to say: 'That high lobbing ball of young McDonagh's was the one that did for us! Well done, Father Joe and the Seminary! But dang blast ye anyway for putting an end to our chances!'

As he stood there besides the posts, Father Joe was a-tremble with excitement, lifting up his toes inside his mud-spotted black shoes and rocking back and forth on his heels at the same time. 'Into the square!' barked young Mike McQuillan as his voice rolled out across the field and the sodden ball came freefalling towards his outstretched arms. 'What a powerful bunch of men!', thought the priest to himself. 'As solid a team of dedicated lads as ever this college has seen pass through its portals!' Which must have been true, for exactly when a college team had made it so far in the Leinster championships, Father Joe certainly couldn't remember. And had it worked wonders for seminary morale? It was amazing what success in the field of sport could do for contemplative young men in terms of comradeship and spirit. It was as if the entire building was emitting a spiritual electric light that radiated throughout the dormant, lassitudinous countryside. With each kick of the ball, a young Man's voice crying out: 'We shall lead! We, the holy and dedicated your men of this seminary shall sally forth and show you, solid, labouring peasant folk of our little country, the way to peace and love in the fellowship of The Sacred Heart!' It was a long time since Father Joe had been so content. As he stood there in the flapping wind, he whispered a silent prayer to St Joseph of Cupertino who, strictly speaking, was the patron saint of examinations, and did not concern himself with sport, but to whom the priest had always had a special devotion, that they might achieve victory by a substantial margin this coming Saturday in Borris-in-Ossory football ground.

It was exactly this thought which was in the mind of nineteen-year-old-student and footballer Bernard McIvor of the townland of Drumaloon, Tyreelin, as he made his way towards the sideline now that the final whistle had been blown, so many premutations and possibilities of the forthcoming game being played out in his imagination that it was almost exhausting. But, as his friend, Dermot Faughnan, observed in the showers as the spiky sprays of steam pelted all about them—leaping frantically off their gleaming flesh, 'All we can do this Saturday, Bernard, is to give our best and play our hearts out isn't it?'

'It is indeed, Dermot,' replied the student priest as he applied the soap to the underside of his private parts, instinctively turning his face away as he always did, least somehow he might instigate once more that gathering movement within those regions, which, in his own mind, he was wont to call the '*bad thing*'. And which the sport of football was absolutely wonderful for, because when you were soaring high into the air to catch the laced-up leather orb which was often wet and soggy (but who cared!), you simply didn't think of girls in diaphanous dresses or even mature women in foundation garments who came visiting nocturnally to part their lips and say those things to you. Things that you didn't want to hear. Things that they pretended were quite innocent, of course, Like: 'Hello, Bernard' or 'It's quiet in here, isn't it, Bernard? In this dormitory, I mean!' Ever so foxily too, of course, delivering it in such a seemingly innocuous way that you would never be able to say back to them: 'You'd better stop this now! I know what you're trying to do to me! *I* know what you're trying to do to me, Miss! Or Mrs!—'

Turn around and put the blame on you, if you see what I mean! Insisting: 'What? But I didn't say anything! What I said was perfectly harmless, for heaven's sake! You can't turn around and blame me just because your tootle takes it upon itself to salute me the way it's doing!' Which wasn't a nice thing to do—well, not so much 'not nice', maybe—but definitely not fair. It wasn't fair to say those things to Bernard when he was all alone in bed and, what's more, so utterly defenceless. It wasn't as if it was the fullback of St Malachy's he was facing or the so-called brilliant winger Matt McGlinchey! Them he could face no bother! Pluck the ball off their toes and with it run like the wind! But, when someone stood before you, just standing there and going: 'Hello, Bernard!', what were you supposed to do, particularly if a little breeze fluttered up the diaphanous material and made you see—*oh God! Oh, no! God help me! Oh Jesus Christ!*'

It was quite common for student priests to awake some minutes before the actual peal of the morning bell. It is a habit they acquire. It is a habit which is good, providing you as it does with some moments to reflect upon the day which is about to come. A short time in which to privately commune with your Saviour to whom you have effectively dedicated your life. None of which is relevant in this case, as Bernard has been awake not for some moments but since 3 A.M. And is in quite a state, I'm afraid. It is as if his life has entered a new, potentially deadly phase. For, if the nocturnal visitations of Foundation Garments and Diaphanous were a source of dread which he valiantly attempted to dispel with his multifarious bull-like charges into the wind on so many football fields, what new strategies could he employ to negotiate the wiles of the one in whose black and whirlpool eyes he had hopelessly swum, nay flailed. And who like a snake had svelte-slid from his bed with the words: 'Same time tomorrow night, darling,' to vanish then beneath the crucifix of the Saviour who from the blankness of the wall reproached him with huge sadness, before he could even utter the words he wished to say to her: 'No! Not tomorrow night! Or any night! Go away! Go away for ever!'

Was it any wonder his bedsheets were practically liquefied, what with the perspiration and other unnamable body fluids. Not least of which streamed so long and hard they might well have had as their geneses the extirpations of entire continents. 'Why! Why! Why!' he chided himself as he dabbed those undryable eyes with a twisted little spear of the sodden bedsheet. 'Because you failed!' the Saviour replied, with a stony expression that would chill your blood, because of course you rarely saw it on the selfless face,

122

'Because you fell!' And no baby ever cried, in a lonely dormitory or anywhere else, as did that once dying-to-be-a-priest boy named Bernard McIvor. Who, from that day on, summoned all his resources to face those silkfloating apparitions which late in the nights came to blink their spectral pools again and whisper and who, even after, to this end, devoted himself almost entirely to prayer and spiritual reading (*Restraint And Denial—A Handbook For Clergymen*).

*

None of which proved any good, did it, when one frosty unspectacular morning his new young housekeeper who resembled Mitzi Gaynor leaned across the table to give him his breakfast (Ah! Yummy rashers! Eggs too! Powerful!) and set off an atomic explosion in those serge trunks once again, with the result that his spiritual reading had all come to nothing, a thought no doubt shared by the bubble-cut girl now pinned against the wall, wondering what exactly was going on down there in that place where only moments before she'd found herself but somehow now had floated far away!

*

When Terence came in I was screaming his name (Daddy's—Bernard's—whatever the fuck you want to call him) and was tearing the pages into pieces, crying: 'I'll fucking kill him! I'll cut his fucking cock off and burn his church down with him in it!'

The blood was pulsing in my head so fast I thought I'd get a haemorrhage. Only for old oaken-arms I probably would have! He gave me tea and calmed me down and told me what I'd have to learn.

'You'll have to learn to forgive,' he said. 'For if you don't, you know what will happen?'

'What, Doctor?' I croaked, for my outburst had exhausted me.

'It will destroy you,' he said as he handed me the tea.

A tear came into my eye when he said it for I knew it was true and I would have loved to be able to do it (not because of its destroying me but because it was right, and deep down I knew that) but I couldn't and the more I thought of it the more the blood came coursing to my head so that whenever I'd write I'd find myself clutching the pencil so tight I broke the lead how many times I don't know, hundreds.

Chapter Thirty-Three

A Long-Ago Night in November

Mr And Mrs Johnny Bergin loved Saturday night. Especially in November when you could look out at the frost starching the beautiful countryside rigid, as you thought to yourself: 'Isn't it lovely to be in here now with a big fire on, listening to the wireless and not a thing to worry you now you've been to confession and the good Lord is looking down on you thinking: "Now there's the Bergins—I'm pleased with them!"'

Which was only right and proper, for in all of Tyreelin, you would not have found nicer, decenter people than the Bergin family. Mr. Bergin's eyelids were drooping a little but as he sat in the armchair, partly because of the hypnotic motion of the flames in the grate but also because he had been working hard all day on the new estate of houses which was going up at the edge of the village. Mrs Bergin smiled as she looked over at him, then went back to reading her Sacred Heart Messenger. She was reading the thoughts of St Anthony. He was her favourite saint. How many prayers she had said to him over the years, only God Himself would have been able to say. And not one of them had she ever regretted, as she often remarked to her neighbours. 'Any safety pin I ever lost, any shilling coin or prayer-book—good St Anthony always helped me find it.' As she thought that again now, she rested her hands on her lap and whispered another little silent prayer. Outside, a dog barked and then all was quiet again throughout the village. She smiled to herself as she heard her only daughter moving about upstairs, and thought then of her little boy James, as he would have been, who had been born dead a year before Eileen. How wonderful it would have been to have watched them grow up together, James at his football and Eily (as everyone affectionately called her) at her music. For how she just loved music. As her husband Johnny had often said: 'How it doesn't put her astray in the head, I don't know! For I couldn't listen to it!' But that was her life, wasn't it? As soon as she had her books done—it was straight up the stairs to put on those records of hers that she bought for 1/6 in McKeon's shop and leaf though the magazines—*Picturegoer, Screen Parade, New Faces of the Fifties*—God bless us, where did she get them all? But sure what harm did it do? Didn't the nuns tell her if she kept at her work the way she was going, she might well end up at the university, and how many Tyreelin girls had ever been able to say that? Which was why, when she heard the floorboards above her creak and the strains of Vic Damone singing '*Stay With Me*', or '*On the Street Where You Live*' coming down the stairs, Mrs Bergin just went on with her sewing and stitching and said to herself: 'That's Eily.' 'Which is exactly what she said when the occasional neighbour remarked: 'You don't mind her going to these hops every Thursday, Mrs?' 'I do not,' she says. 'For that's Eily.' Who, from the day she had been able to walk, had never uttered a cross word to her mother. And who hadn't the slightest hesitation in agreeing to help out Sister Lorcan when she told her of Mrs McGlynn's (the priest's house-keeper) mishap. 'Wasn't she coming down the hill from the presbytery—you know what the frost's been like—and didn't she go and slip outside Pat McCrudden's gate!' In fact, what she had said was that she would be more than glad to assist Father Bernard in Mrs McGlynn's absence—especially when it was only a matter of making his breakfast, and doing one or two other chores.

Which she now deeply regretted, of course. Except that her mother didn't know it. Had noted, it is true, her daughter's seeming lack of interest in record-buying and her suspension of attendance at the hops for which she once would have truly died. And which to Eily herself seemed to have begun almost a thousand years ago now, although it was only a matter of months. Since she had strolled through the streets of the village with her house-coat on underneath her back coat and her check scarf tied around her head, thinking: 'If I save up all the money Father Bernard gives me, I'll be able to buy the top ten records in the hit parade.' And who knew—perhaps even the long player of the film *South Pacific*!

'I love Rosanno Brazzi,' she said to herself as she walked past Mulvey's pub. 'I love him and I love his music.'

The music she had been singing to as she fished around in the foaming suds of the presbytery kitchen wash-hand basin for her broken fingernail. 'After all—we don't want Father Bernard to get it in his breakfast!' she laughed to herself. Just as she felt the tips of his fingers brushing against ever so slightly as he went past, never for even a sec-ond thinking to herself: 'I know what that means! It's just a prelude to later on in the parlour, isn't it, when he's going to come after me with that great big screaming stalker of his!'

As indeed—why should she? Which is a pity, all the same, for at least then it might have made some sense to her, being pinned up there against the wall—with a forty-year-old clergyman sliding his tootle in and out of her at a furious rate of knots. 'Who is this girl?' She kept asking herself as she looked down from a height at the creature whose head kept bumping off the table leg. It wasn't her, that was for sure, for she kept pleading: 'Stop! Stop!' It was obviously someone else, someone else who looked like her. She hoped it wouldn't upset her, that she might not regret it some day. Because Eily knew that was what it did, that sort of conduct. Her mother had told her. Not in so many words, of course. And especially—most especially with a priest—even if it was the priest's fault. All Eily could think was: 'I'm glad it's not me!' Because she was saving herself for marriage. She might dance at the hops and everything but marriage to her was something pure and clean and wholesome. White as driven snow. Not at all like what Father Bernard was doing right now. That wasn't it at all. Why was he doing it, though? she wondered. It made her cry to watch him as he continued.

But not as much as it made her cry when she realised just who it was, i.e. that it had been her all along! You can imagine the shock she got. Crying: 'Why! The girl *is* me!' and then of course, the baby coming—the biggest shock of all!

What it would have been like if her mammy'd known or somehow seen behind the big clothes, she could only imagine. Indeed, in her mind, already had done many times seeing her mother's face to the fore of the throng in the middle of Tyreelin Square, the faces twisted with a hatred she had never before seen. Her own mother joining in with them as they cried: 'Hang her! Hang the bitch!' and Eily Bergin dangled from a lamp-post. It was silly, of course. It could never happen! It was just her imagination working overtime! What was she going to do? Giddily she thought: 'What should I do? Scoop it out with a wooden spoon perhaps?' That made her laugh. 'I might only get its eye,' she said, spluttering mucus into her hand.

In the end, the baba slid out nice and easy. On that very November evening when Mr and Mrs Bergin were sitting cosily by the nice log fire. Not exactly at that time, but a few hours later, in the early hours of the morning. What Eily could not get over was—one minute, there's nothing there and the next—a whole human being! With little thin arms and little thin legs and soft browny hair and an oval face. And looking so yummy! 'I want to keep him! I want to keep my baby!' she wanted to howl. But she couldn't do that!

Anyway, Father Bernard had told her what must be done. He'd been so nice and kind at the end of it all. In the beginning he'd been nasty. 'You're not keeping it! Are you mad?' he'd bellowed like a bull. She thought he was even going to hit her. Especially when she cried.

'Stop it! Your hear! Stop that crying now!' Having to shake her until she stopped! Which was silly of her—she knew that now. After all, she was sixteen. It was time she saw sense.

As she did now, once more strolling though the streets but this time with her Rinso box of baba tucked beneath her arm. Obviously, she was terrified she was going to meet someone—such as Sonny Macklin on his way to work, perhaps. 'Where are going with that box, Eily?' Or even worse—who knew? 'Lets have a look at what you have inside there!'

It was hard not to cry but she had bought lots of tissues and, in any case, by the time she reached Ma Braden's, she wasn't quite so bad. Most of her tears had dried away. So she just left baby in his box and then went off for ever. But where did she go? No one knows! Was she killed in an accident? Did the holyhead ferry sink? Why—it's a mystery!

Poor old Mr Bergin—he went out of his mind, you know! You'd be out walking and you'd come across him talking to a cow. 'I don't know if I told you or not, but my Eily—she's a divil for these pop records. God bless us and save us, to see her up in that room of hers, dancing—you'd have to ask: "What's the world coming to?" '

Mrs Bergin it didn't bother for so long and when the stroke took her away, everyone said it was good, which in a way it was.

So that morning, and in particular the part of it between 3.00 and 3.20 A.M., was not what you'd call a good one for anyone.

Except Hairy Braden the Baby Farmer, of course—for whom it meant twenty pounds a month—sometimes twenty-five!

Not that there'd be much of a chance of Hairy showing gratitude, pulling up the leg of her drawers, dragging on the cigarette-holed dressing gown and flinging the door open before sweeping up the cardboard box and standing there as she whistled through crevassed teeth: 'Another hooring beggar's get!' as poor Puss went: '*Miaow!*'

Chapter Thirty-Four

The Life and Times of Pat Puss, Hooker

As she did for all and sundry now, so sky-high giddy since she'd left Louise's she seemed to work non-stop! 'O please, please, buy me sweet Chanel!' to some hunk she now would cry, as lashings of cash upon her were laid and her kohl-rimmed eyes misted over with desire as into hipster trouser suits she slipped, blouson tops and milkmaid maxis, enough to drive her poor man wild! 'O miaow, my darling!' she cried. 'So kind to Pussy are you that I really, truly must adore you as no lady ever did!'

And so each night, jangly-bangly, whiff of No. 5 ('Gosh! You like your perfume!' often he would say), in knee boots she'd come tripping, Aubrey-bob lacquered in place. So high was she, what pray is that, so many miles below—'Why! The city of London it is, methinks!', all winking with its signals trying to reach sweet Pussy and say: 'Come back to earth!' but no—'Methinks I've had enough of that!', she cries—then when words with Charlie on the phone she did swop—it never quite dawned on her that Irwin was dead. Although she'd heard it many times, for Charlie couldn't stop repeating it. As she'd been doing since he died, having really gone quite mad!

'I'll see you, darling!' was all Puss said. 'I've got to go—a client! Toodle-oo!'

You would have to ask—was Puss gone too, to that nutty no-rule place? The question must be asked!

As it was by dearest Terence (Bastard! Go on—leave me! No, I don't mean that!) who said: 'So to all intents and purposes you were living as a woman now?'

'Well, I didn't have any yucky briefs if that's what you mean, my sweet!' said Puss and chuckled in her chuckly way, her head as light as air.

'Sometimes they'd ask me to do my Dusty.' She'd smile and roll her eyes, wondering was it something Tersey too did fancy. 'I'd dance for them and husky-coo until they could take no more. And other times—'

'Other times?'

'Why I'd be a right old whore!'

As Tersey's cheeks went pinky. Yes! They truly did!

And gave me courage! I went over to him and stocked his cheek. Then dropped my eyelids and sexy-whispered: 'Before I became a bomber, of course!'

It was hard not to laugh—because he took it so serious! Which he had to—as indeed I ought to—after all, people lost their limbs and eyes!

But I couldn't, Pussy as a bomber—I simply had to clutch my sides!

Chapter Thirty-Five

Detention in the School of
Dr Vernon, Late October 1974

It is four o'clock in the afternoon in the Earl's Court Hotel School and Dr Vernon is not pleased. 'I distinctly told you to be here at three forty-five!' he says to Mandy his pupil— (Pussy in disguise, of course! Sporting pigtails—can you believe it! More fiendish money-making schemes!)—who now she hangs her head in shame.

'Yes,' she replies, 'I know that. I know that, Dr Vernon. But—'

'Not buts!' he hissed and he looks so cross, it has to be for a split-second considered he might well be another Silky String. O no, please, no!

Fortunately, however, not the case! As he peremptorily intones:

'You are perfectly aware that punishment for tardiness at the Earl's Court Academy is strangling by ligature, are you not. . . . ?' O no! But not to be—

*

Dr Vernon is much nicer than old Silks could ever be! He

just makes you do one hundred lines. And paces around as you write them:

I Must Not be a Bad Mandy.
I Must Not be a Bad Mandy.

Then, what does he do? Brings you off to the restaurant for a great big yummy din dins!

And then to Harrods to by you hundreds of frou-frou fluffies—including an explosion of white fur with the shortest back dress ever—not to mention the fabbest Chanel-y suit, Saxone shoes and a delicious peach satin shirt! Oh, how you exult! How one squeaks with pure delight!

Then making a silly mistake—moving in with old silly Vernon! 'I want to be your husband!' The great old idiot! I couldn't stand him after a while! 'Shall we go to Sainsbury's? That should be quite exciting! Or perhaps I ought to wash the car! Yes—that's what I shall do!'

O and did I become a broody bitch! Which was why I left! Went running out the door—again!—in fact, the minute I got the chance!

Chapter Thirty-Six

Al Pacino Reveals All!

O and why would I not be a happy girl walking around this glitter-night in London's glorious West End— *'Oh, Calcutta! Now in its fourth year!'*, *'The Exorcist!'* ('Your mother cooks socks in hell—ha ha!'), *'Carry On London—At Last! They're carrying on—live on stage!'* (Ooh, matron! Distinctly said, 'Prick his boils did you? I am sorry!')—and I am not going back to my husband Vernon because you see I don't love him any more and I don't see why you should have to live with someone you don't love. One day soon I will write him a letter and say, dear Vernon, darling, I am sorry I have not come home. You are a very sweet man and I love you dearly but not in the way that a wife should love her husband so I think it is only fair and honest to tell you this so that you can find someone to love and care for you the way you deserve. I want to thank you too for all the beautiful things you bought me, especially this lovely ice-cream pink mohair sweater and black pleated skirt which goes so well with my black suede knee boots. I am sure you can imagine how good I feel as I swing my Gucci shoulder bag (bought by you too, sweetness, I'm afraid!) and let myself be swallowed up by the flashing console colours of this most wondrous city. There are parties on tonight, my darling. As you might expect, considering it's coming up to Christmas. If she looks into this restaurant, through this frosted glittering glass, what does Patrick Puss-divorced-from-dearest-Vernon now see? A sea of shining faces and glasses raised on high. '*And I said to her, I said—if you expect me to—*', as girls flick back their hair. Not really listening! Having too good a time!

As merry crowds now surge though streets of white cut-stone that vibrate in the night, past Piccadilly railings opposite Eros and near the Wimpy where they expect to see young Puss tonight. Except, she isn't selling! Too soft and frail, and fragile maybe too! Wants it all over, I'm afraid! Just wants to settle down, safe and snug beneath an arm so big and bearlike. Silly Puss-Puss, Max Factor Miss with lots of men who want yum yum! But not the way she does! The way they do in *Loving* magazine! O!, she sighs, if it could only be!

PUSSY—MY LIFELONG PARTNER
AL PACINO REVEALS ALL!

Sweet he is, but for Puss it cannot be. Rock stars catching planes will only make you weep. Her man to be loved for ever and ever but only by Pussy catkins Swing-the-Bag!

—Only by me and no one else!

Dear Cathy and Claire:
I want to be married to a real man. A Rock. Can you help me?

Dear Pussy Willow Poo Poos searching for a Man:
We thought YOU could help US!

'Sigh!' thinks Puss Puss, wondering aloud:

—What can the future hold? What, what, what can the future hold, now my tootling days are at an end?

Not knowing that right at that moment, that very second somewhere deep in darkest Cricklewood, moves were already afoot to send her flying towards it, with some gusto!

*

(Terence said: 'Did you imagine all this, Patrick! Or were you actually at some point involved with these bombers?'

I ought to have played him along a little—it would have been fun just teasing him! Instead of saying, all coyly like I did: 'Oh, Terence! Don't start pretending my writing skills are that good!')

But you could still see him looking at me—*Pussy! Mad Bomber!* Could it be true?

O Terence! Honestly—for heaven's sake! Sometimes I wonder how I ever fell for you!

137

Chapter Thirty-Seven

Busy Men Prepare to Blow Up London and Get Pussy into Trouble

It was six o'clock—6th November, 1974 and Big Joe Kiernan from Offaly was smoking a Player's No. 6 cigarette and simultaneously humming '*My Ding A Ling*' by Chuck Berry as his nicotine-stained fingers doubled the end of a piece of copper wire from which he had removed the plastic coating and inserted it though the hole he had made in the glass of the pocket watch, flicking the cigarette away as he taped the wire into place. His companion, the man everyone called Mayo Jack, although it wasn't his real name, was humming a tune too but was completely unaware of it, absorbed by the photo story which he was reading in a copy of *True Detective* magazine. Every so often he would read a little bit of it out and the third man, who had only recently arrived from Belfast, would say: 'Och, you're away in the head, Jack!' and then go back to frying his chops on the pan. His name was Faigs—because he was always asking for cigarettes, of course, as in: 'Have youse any faigs?' and it was his job to plant all the bombs from now on because Tinker—who had been doing it up to now—had gone back to Dublin. Now that the six sticks of gelignite were taped down and the parcel more or less ready, there wasn't very much else for Big Joe to do only play darts until Faigs was ready. They were in a hurry to get going and tried to chivvy him on a little but it was no use. Until he was good and ready, you just wouldn't be getting Faigs McKeever going anywhere. 'Away and give my head peace!' was the only response their coaxing received from him. 'Oh, go and fuck yourself then!' Big Joe said as a green-feathered dart sailed expertly towards the measled corkboard. In all, they managed to have three games before Faigs actually declared himself ready. 'Took your fucking time!' said Jack as he picked up the leatherette holdall they'd just put the bomb in. 'Don't forget your magazine,' Faigs chuckled as he winked at the *femme deshabillée* on the cover and grabbed his friend between the legs, Mayo Jack hitting him with two well-aimed jabs and laughing: 'Fuck you!' as Big Pat opened the door of the brown Mark 2 Ford Cortina and climbed inside.

Chapter Thirty-Eight

Ooh, Bomber!

Pie-eyed though she was (Camparis in Soho all day!), Pussy knew she was being very cheeky indeed when she got it into her head to pop into the disco-pub which was jam-packed full of soldiers. But she didn't care—so what if she'd had a few drinkies and if anyone as much as said boo to her, why she would just laugh in their faces. 'Oh! So I'm a man, am I? Full marks for observation, sweetie!' she fully intended to say if that proved to be the case—big tough soldiers or no!

Which it probably would, of course—as well in her heart she knew, for it seemed as if every squaddie in the country had decided to do some shaky-bootie in London town tonight! Perfectly fine by Puss! O but yes and more than fine! For, who knew—perhaps she might meet Sergeant Rock or Captain Yum Yum Be-My-Girl-For-Ever! And if the risk was not worth that, then life, she whispered to herself, it simply was not worth the living.

In any case, there was a strong chance he might not know the truth. An hour in the hotel loo had seen to that, with her long brown hair now so gleamy and her glossy lips a-shining! Then, straight through the door to watch those swooning soldier boys!

As the strobe lights swept across her, Barry White was smooching: 'You're The First, The Last, My Everything!' and tingle-tingly went Puss down in the groin, the short-haired squaddie whispering in her ear: 'You fancy a drink or summat?' Puss coughing a little to summon up the courage to whisper, squeaky-voiced: 'Oh, yes!' and look into his eyes when one part of his head went to the left, the other part to the right and the brains which were inside to the floor pouring like scrambled egg—or so it seemed to Puss. The squaddie was definitely dead—I mean, there was blood all over his face, and he was lying on the floor. It was as if it never at any time occurred to Pussy to move. Standing there as if still waltzing with an invisible soldier, where she had been, she compliantly remained.

At least a minute had passed before it dawned on her that she wasn't dead too. 'I'm not dead,' she said, and touched her lipstick with the tip of her tongue. She couldn't taste anything. 'Strange,' she mused to herself, 'I can't taste anything at all.' It was only then she noticed her Christian Dior tights were torn to ribbons. All around her, she slowly began to discern, lots of things were flying. There were particles of sawdust, grit and scraps of paper. If anyone had been observing Puss, they would surely have said: 'Why is she laughing, for heaven's sake? Doesn't she realize she ought to be dead?' Which, if they'd asked her, they would have soon found out that was precisely the cause of her thin, protracted laugh—the fact that it was dawning on her that she must have been practically beside the point of detonation. What she was doing there—standing up, fingering her gold neck chain and thinking: 'I must be practically beside the point of detonation and my tights are in ribbons. I must get a new pair! I really must!' It was while Pussy was repeating this that there was another explosion nearby and a dazzling flash of blue light through which white faces rushed before being engulfed by a wave of intense heat. As she played with the necklace, Pussy continued to be oblivious of the proceedings—a motorcyclist blown off his machine as static spurted into the shattered night: '*Priority! Priority!*' A strip of nylon from Puss's tights had become detached and looked for all the world like a scorched piece of skin hanging from the cheek of one of the dead soldiers. It wasn't the one Pussy had been dancing with. It was someone else. There were lots. Puss shouldn't have laughed when the first policeman on the scene tugged at a woman's leg only to find it coming away in his hand. But because she had gone sky-high giddy again, she couldn't help it. She kept thinking of the bobby in the childhood comics and that at any moment he was going to scratch his head, then shake it and say: 'Well, blow me, sarge! They've gone and scarpered again!'

Which of course attracted no end of attention to her, as if she was taking pleasure in the poor man's misfortune, still doing it when they were dragging her out and calling her 'a facking cow!' and 'Irish bitch!' and God knows what else because they were, understandably, furious!

Even more so when in the hospital they discovered her little secret, Puss of course not doing an absolute thing to explain the situation, not even bothering to raise a blackened (well, actually, it wasn't—that bit is fanciful—as Terence well spotted!) finger and say: 'No! You don't quite get

142

it! You see, what I am is an ordinary transvestite prostitute, not the slightest bit interest in politics at all!' Far too worried about her lovely ice-cream pink mohair sweater and gorgeous black pleated mini-skirt to be even bothered in fact. Which was a very serious mistake indeed, as it turned out, for after two or three conversations with her, nothing would convince them that the baby-faced male bomber they now had firmly in their grasp was anything other than a wicked little fucker who would stop at nothing in his determination to mutilate and maim, even going so far as to disguise himself as a tart, a piece of information which they had no hesitation in giving to the papers who by now of course were screaming to high heaven for a conviction.

To this day I regret that I didn't keep the *Daily Mirror* and the *Sun*, for I didn't look at all bad in either! Even when scorched and sky-high giddy! (The policemen had to tell me to shut up when they were taking the photo!)

They let me hold on to a copy and all that second night I couldn't resist taking it out and looking at it, spluttering into my hands ever time I'd see the bold black type: '*Sweet Smile of a Killer*!', which was hilarious, it really was, particularly with the glazy look I had in my eyes and my clothes ripped to shreds. Especially, as I say, my Christian Diors! Which they had arrows pointing to so you could see my hairy legs. 'O there's no doubt about it!' I'd say, whenever they brought me in my meals. 'It really is hilarious!'

But, as I said to Terence, not quite so hilarious when Detective Inspector Routledge and his good pal Police Constable Wallis started shoving me around the shop! All I can say is, if you weren't whistling Dixie backwards on the far side of Pluto by the time they were finished with you, dearies, then you were made of strong stuff and no mistake—which, sorry to say, Miss Pussy wasn't!

Why, she even stopped being a cigarette paper, I think, and became nothing so much as dusty fragments blowing every which way right out there across the vast unending firmament!

Which probably explained why for no reason she would laugh in what were all the wrong places—because she simply didn't know! After all, it must be accepted that it is quite difficult to pinpoint places back on earth when you are somewhere in the region of 2.5 billion miles from it. Which Puss, and more than once, in fact, did actually state. 'I'm sorry!', she said with her giddy laugh that was really driving them quite wild now, 'I can't see you all down there, I'm afraid! Where are you?'

'Don't try any of your fucking blarney on us, Paddy!', PC Wallis would say then, with his face right into hers—and his eyes quite mad! 'We know you planted that bomb!'

To which Puss, chuckle-heaving did reply: 'But of course I did, my darling! Of course I did—and have planted hundreds!

As Wallis to his full height now rose up, puffed out with pride to say: 'I told you so!'

Whereupon Puss from the chair she fell and foetus-crouched and squealed!

Chapter Thirty-Nine

'It's Bombing Night and I haven't Got a Thing to Wear'

It is a quiet Thursday evening in the London suburb of Hammersmith and the IRA active service unit was getting ready for another night on the town. All week they had been busy and been so successful were now considering returning to the branch of Fortnum and Mason which they had reduced to rubble only days before. But, after much discussion, this was decided against and instead everyone plumped for a salubrious West End restaurant where stockbrokers and members of parliament were known to dine. As soon as the decision had been made, everyone set to work, applying themselves to the tasks which by now were second nature. First there was gelignite to be unwrapped—with special care of course—after all, we didn't want anyone to be getting nitroglycerine sickness (or 'NG Head' as the lads called it), the hands to be clipped off pocket watches and the one hundred and one different things that you had to do when you were on active service. Paddy Pussy, of course, being the undisputed leader of the unit, was well-occupied too, slipping into one of his many luxurious evening

gowns—this particular one bias-cut, in pink satin crepe—
and posing literally for hours in front of the mirror, trying
to establish once and for all just how good he looked on this
momentous occasion, the first time he had actually bombed
a restaurant in the city of London. Up until now, it had mostly
been assorted public buildings, and tube stations of course.

'Oh, figs!', she exclaimed, casting her fifteenth and
final gown to the floor. 'Let someone else do it tonight! I
can't find a thing to wear!

'No! No, please!', the other members of the unit pleaded
with their adored leader. 'We beg you to do it, Puss! After
all, you are the most feared terrorist in London!'

'Oh, don't I know it, sweetie!' cried Pussy, as she
flapped her hands. 'Don't I just know it, all you flattering,
sweety honey pies!'

An Out-of-Body Experience Perhaps?

Terence said to me: 'Did you have an out-of-body experience when you were incarcerated in that cell, Patrick, do you think, for it certainly seems as if you weren't there much!'

It was just his sense of humour coming out when he said that but I know what he meant! As I'm sure poor old Wallis and Routledge did when they'd look through the Judas Hole and there I'd be, tittering and laughing to myself, all these thoughts along with me out in space, as I considered everything that had happened up to now and how I was going to make everyone sorry. 'For what?' says Routledge, when they eventually gave up their sniggering and came in to see me. 'Oh, don't worry!' I says, and spluttered laughing all over again! 'Fuck!' says Routledge, kicking the table. 'Fucking fucking fuck!'

Chapter Forty

A Lot of People Losing It!

Detective Inspector Peter Routledge of Scotland Yard Criminal Investigation Department was at his wit's end, pacing the floor of the dayroom relentlessly as he cracked his knuckles and smoked endless cigarettes. For four days now he had been holding his suspect—the maximum of course was seven days—and it had already got to the stage where he could get nothing out of him but complete and utter nonsensical gibberish. Why would he just not talk? Why could he not just admit he had dressed up as a woman in an ingenious scheme to disguise himself—for they would stop at nothing, these mad, fanatical bombers—and his plan had gone horribly wrong! What was the matter with these people—that this 'cause' of theirs could inspire them to go out and commit these crimes against humanity—leaving young women without legs, human beings scarred for ever both physically and psychologically? Who would blame him for 'losing it' as his colleague had termed it, when he had seen and heard the laughter of that lunatic bastard in the cell when confronted with the photographs of those he had disfigured and destroyed—all because of politics!

'Politics!' snapped the inspector. 'I'll facking give 'im

politics!', and was about to return to the cell to knock some more sense into his suspect, actually having to be physically restrained by Wallis who cried:

'For God's sake, Peter! Get a grip of yourself, man! If you lose it again—!'

'I'm not losing it! I'm not going to sit there watching that little cant making fun of us—I'll facking kill 'im!'

What was at the back of the inspector's mind, of course, gnawing away at him like cancer, was the nagging suspicion that he might have apprehended the wrong person. What if the callow, fair-skinned youth (David Cassidy—we love you!) was, in fact, as he insisted, nothing more than a drifting transvestite prostitute from the backwoods of Ireland, in search of nothing more than a good time and a reasonable living on the streets of London? A cold sweat broke out of his skin and he shuddered, considering for the tiniest fraction of a second the possibility that had been advanced by his colleague, that the youth, far from being someone possessing the personality of steel which enabled him to disregard everything they said with what appeared to be cheerful disdain, was quite the opposite, as indeed might be the nature of his laughter. Which really ought to have suggested to him, in some form or another, the thought: 'I don't think I'm the only one losing it around here, constable! To tell you the truth, I think there are a lot of people!'

But didn't, I'm afraid! The silly man just kept on shouting more and more!

Chapter Forty-One

Hello, Mrs Braden!

And who was it within my darkened cellbox upon whom mine eyes did gladly fall as there I sat sky-high a-twiddle, ringed around by stars and planets? Why, the one and only Eily Bergin, of course, clear as day behind that shining light that now surrounded her, making her way to a certain house at the back end of Tyreelin to utter at last those famous words: 'Hello, Mrs Braden! I'm pleased to meet you! I want my son. May I have him, please?'

And what would old Hairy have to say to that? Disgruntedly plucking me from the snotnosed posse and, turning her arse to the wind, declare: 'Here—take him! For all the good he's ever been round here!'

Well, what fun we would have then, me and the woman I'd dreamt about those thousand nights and one in the choking den called Rat Trap Mansions. 'Mammy!', I would say to her as down the street in sunshine we two made our way. 'Do you think I'm the way I am because Daddy's work makes him wear those dresses?'

Which would make her laugh and say: 'Of course not, silly, You simply wear them because that's just how you are!' And what would I say then? 'How's that for a mammy!' and rasp at all the snot-nosed urchins who now did line the road seething with unbridled jealousy. Mumbling to their tattered mothers: 'His Mum's a Lady!'

Absolutely true, of course! Why, for all the world she'd look like Sophia Loren! Chewing the stem of her Polaroids!

And boy what fun there truly now would be! Together out across the stars, all the time in the universe ours, making up for all we'd lost. And going where we'd want to!

Chapter Forty-Two

Vengeance Shall Be Mine, Says Puss!

To a desert island, even, right there in the cell, one that now belonged to us and forever would be ours! Unseen by Wallis, Routledge, of course! Who nothing spied but a raggedy-edged old Pussy rolling around the floor—when she wasn't picking plaster from the wall emitting moans of exultation truly inexplicable! On one occasion even calling: 'Mammy!'

'Fuck this!', muttered Detective Inspector Routledge to himself as he shoved the receiver into its cradle. 'I need a holiday, away from all this fucking insanity!'

Which makes one wonder what he'd have thought if he'd seen where Pussy and Mumsy had landed now! Prostrate beneath a bending palm, on an infinite stretch of powder sand. 'O Mammy!' said Puss as he hugged her arm and she ran her fingers through his hair. Far away in the distance, a tiny porpoise rose and came down curving in the blue. Close by, the lush vegetation made a hushing sound that was all its own. Colour-splashed across the trees, the parakeets began an unholy racket.

'They're worse than the Tyreelin women,' Eily said, and Pussy laughed. Then she looked at him and said: 'I love you, Pussy.'

She looked adorable in her mango-and-banana-motif swimsuit. 'An awful lot better than me,' thought Puss as he considered his own plain, unpatterned affair, the only exciting feature of which was its delicate spaghetti straps.

'Pussy,' she said then, 'wasn't he really an awful person to do what he did?'

'Who—Father Bernard?' he said, and she nodded.

'Yes. He was, Mammy,' he replied and felt his cheeks go hot—as hot as the sun that was rising over Bali Ha'ai.

'But it's a long time ago,' she said as she looked into his eyes. 'And we've got to forget. Somehow we've got to forget and forgive.'

It was the kindness in those eyes that made him weep then, Pussy. And the knowledge that no matter how he tried, he never would be able.

'I can't, Mammy!' he cried, and got into quite a state. 'I can't you see! I've tried and tried!'

*

When Routledge and Wallis came rushing into the cell, they hadn't the faintest idea of course that there was some kind of debate going on on a desert island! All they saw was a teenage bombing suspect bouncing himself off the walls and about to do some serious damage, not to mention repeatedly screaming: 'I'll kill him! I'll kill him! I'll burn his church and him along with it! They'll pay, you'll see! All of them!' before slipping to the floor and whimpering for a while. If he'd thus remained, they would have been happy, for sedatives meant they lost a day, perhaps two or more, but which the doctor said were absolutely necessary—as my condition was quite advanced.

Routledge thought that perhaps it was guilt (all the people I'd killed!) and as the town of Tyreelin and my dearest daddy emerged through the fog that enfolded me now, in my bearhugged sleep I called out to him: 'No, Routledge! Anger—anger, don't you see! But listen! For vengeance yet shall be mine!' and watched it all now as it passed before me.

The way all along it ought to have been—put at last to rights by Patrick Pussy, the wrong-to-right avenger!

All the way in her mind from England coming home, a town to take apart! And once and for all to take it away, as though it had never been, the smell and stench that down the generations had a tainted valley filled!

Chapter Forty-Three

The Lurex Avenger

And what fun it would surely be! A lace curtain twitching at a cottage window as a hunted eye comes peeping out and Mrs Whiskers draws back the points to something on the mountain, a silhouette that points its finger and to the breaking light of early dawn does now in husky tones declare: 'To the town of her birth she now returns, to visit every hill and dale, there her mark to leave, not one eye its sight which does retain to say: "I do not see her!" for such will not be possible whilst amongst you now she walks, she who thenceforth shall be called—*The Lurex Avenger!* She who shall be named Stench-Banisher, Perfume-Bringer, Flower-Scatterer, Ender of the Darkness, she who shall wrench this place and the people from the shadows into light!'

Chapter Forty-Four

The Stench That No One Knows Is There

The Nolan Family at No. 39, The Square, Tyreelin, are at the table having tea and not watching telly at all. 'It's silly,' they say, 'this *Some Mothers Do 'Ave 'Em*,' As young Noel says: 'All Frank Spencer does is stupid things. It's the same every week. Who wants to watch that?' 'Yes,' agrees Samantha. 'It's babyish.' Then all set about enjoying their tea. Mum is pouring some tea when she pauses with the pot and says: 'What's that?'

'What's what?' says Dad as his nostrils sniff and twitch and he begins to understand.

'Ugh!' says Mum. 'But where is it coming from?'

It's Chanel No. 19, of course, which I, the Avenger, do absolutely adore! But they do not know from whence it emanates! If mum didn't know better, she'd say to the kids: 'Have you been meddling around in my bedroom upstairs? Stealing my Chanel No. 19?' But she didn't, of course— mainly because she didn't possess any. Wouldn't be caught dead wearing it, in fact! 'O God no!', she often said. 'In fact I rarely wear perfume of any kind!'

Which is a lot more than can be said for Spirit-Pussy, Puss Avenger, as she floats by in the night with great big trails of whiff stringing out behind her like so many silk-blown scarves. It only takes an instant before one's shadow on the blinds is gone and Mummy is saying: 'Hmm. It appears to be gone now. Perhaps we all imagined it!'

'Yes—perhaps we did,' says Dad, although he really doesn't think so at all—he just wants to settle the kids again. As off I go past VG foodstore, petrol pumps and Mulvey's Bar on my travels, having overdone it a little perhaps, but, after all, it is quite a stench that hovers over the village—so long a part of it that no one even knows it's there!

Chapter Forty-Five

A Great Day for Bonzo

Pat McGrane (old classmate) is as happy as Larry. He has just knocked off from his job in Tyreelin Frozen Meats and discovered that he had been given an extra ten pounds in his wage packet, payment for the seven hours he'd worked three weeks previously and completely forgotten about. All he could remember was the foreman asking him would he be able to work extra some week, replying: 'Aye, surely', and then completely forgetting about it. Making those few green notes all the sweeter. Jimmy Hanlon who worked with him on the assembly line went past wiping his hands on his rubber apron and flicking his towel across his shoulder. 'Hello, Pat,' Jimmy said, as Pat acknowledged the greeting with a smile. Folding his pound notes, he placed them neatly in the pocket of his wallet, glowing warmly. Partly because of the infinite possibilities with which the extra remuneration now provided him but more specifically the awareness that it could not have come at a better time, a Thursday evening when he was due, as always, to visit his girlfriend across the border and take her to the Arcadia ballroom where they would dance to Gene Stuart and the Mighty Avons. Whom she loved. Why, he could not for the life of him understand, for as far as he was concerned, Gene Stuart couldn't sing a note. A contention which was the cause of many arguments between them, of course—and ones which Pat always regretted. When they had abated, he would always inwardly chide himself and say: 'Why did I have to contradict her? Why can't I let her alone and allow her to like Gene Stuart if she wants to!' A solemn bond which he would make with himself, only to go and break it all over again the next time she would look up from the paper and say: 'I see Gene Stuart and the Mighty Avons are playing in Forkhill tonight—will we go, Pat?' Hardly would the words have left his lips than he'd find himself saying: 'Gene Stuart? What on earth do you want to see him for?'

He felt an idiot when he did it. But he did it every time! Now, as he motored along in his Anglia, raising an index finger from the steering wheel to acknowledge the passing of Fergus Killen, a neighbour, on his bicycle, he established eye contract with himself in the mirror and committed himself firmly to a reformation of his ways in this respect: 'If Sandra wants to go and see Gene Stuart, then Gene Stuart she shall see. There's going to be no big deal about it, OK?' It would make for a far better night for everyone. In any case, as his conscience insisted, if you weren't prepared to make small compromises like this, what hope was there for a marriage surviving the way it ought to? It was just that he didn't like her kind of music, that was all. 'If only I wasn't such a big Creedence Clearwater Revival fan,' he said to himself. As if there was any hope of that happening!

For Pat simply loved Creedence, and until the day he

died would never understand how people could ever even begin to accept bad versions of their songs by the likes of Gene Stuart. It was because he liked them so much that he had adopted, practically down to the tiniest detail, the style of dress of the lead singer, John Fogerty. Every Thursday night, on would go the lumberjack shirt and denim jeans and what with the identical, collar-length hairstyle (almost Beatlish) and the tiny bootlace tie which he had lately taken to wearing, you would have been hard pressed not to leap to the conclusion that somehow John Fogerty, the lead singer and guitar player of Creedence Clearwater Revival, had arrived in Tyreelin. Over a few pints in Mulvey's, before he went to collect Sandra across the border, Pat's pals would often say: 'Oho, you can traipse about like John Fogerty now, but come your wedding day she'll soon put a stop to all that, I can tell you!' To which Pat might reply: 'Would you go away to fuck out of that!' or 'Do me a fucking favour, lads!'

Driving along now, he smiled as he considered it—knowing in his heart how silly it was. For, whatever about him and Sandra rowing over Gene Stuart, he knew, it would be a long time before she started ordering him around in terms of telling him what to wear and so on. Because, as she had said, God knows how many times, she liked him just the way he was. Loved him, in fact. She had said that too. Playing with the silver clasp on his bootlace tie she had sort of looked away from him as she said it: 'I love you, Pat.' To which it wasn't hard for him to find a response. Because he had been dying to say it all evening, of course. 'I love you too, Sandra,' he said.

Getting ready, he hadn't be able to make up his mind

where they would go before the dance. A lot of the time they went to Hughie's, which was in the middle of the market square in her hometown of Dunkeerin, but of late he had been getting fed up with it and, he suspected, so had she. Hughie's idea of running a pub seemed to be to pack them in and throw any sort of old slops at them. In the middle of the week, it was fine, but on Thursdays it could be a madhouse. Then there was the Spinning Wheel—but that was the opposite. The most exciting thing that happened in there on a Thursday or any other night was someone flicking over a table mat or playing games with matchsticks. It catered more for the bank and teaching crowd—pub grub, soup and sandwiches during the working week, that sort of thing. Then there was Walter's, where you were liable to be taking your life into your hands once you went inside the door. But which could also be worth it if you got in with the right crowd. All the same, Sandra wasn't keen on it. 'No doubt it'll probably end up being McLarnon's again then!' Pat had sighed as he buckled his Levi's belt. Which didn't bother him in the slightest, actually, for they always ended up having a good time there. Sometimes they had good music too—one night a band from Belfast did the most amazing version of 'I Heard It Through the Grapevine'. It had astonished him, in fact, and for weeks after Sandra would say: 'I never seen you looking as entranced, Pat—I really didn't.'

Unfortunately, however, that particular band were nowhere to be seen that night and he and Sandra ended up sitting beside one of the speakers as the singer banged a tambourine and sang: 'Tra la la la la la—triangle!' hopelessly out of tune. But once they got out into the night air,

Pat didn't care. He put his arm around Sandra and kissed her on the mouth. She hooked her thumb into his belt as they walked along. The dance was surprisingly good too and he had even begun to consider he had been unfair to Gene Stuart. Especially when he did a cover of 'Bad Moon Rising'. As they danced, he stroked Sandra's hair and said: 'Come back, Gene Stuart—all is forgiven.'

It was a bit early yet to be talking about the wedding but all the same, there were one or two things which it was no harm to think about—just so as they'd be out of the way. He agreed with her about that. The more they had done beforehand, the easier it would be whenever the planning truly started in earnest. Sandra's mother joined in for a while when they were chatting about it, and actually ended up agreeing with Pat about Gene Stuart—who turned up again in the conversation, completely out of nowhere!

'I can't understand what our Sandra sees in him!' she said and cupped her hand around the blue-striped mug. 'Oh, will you two ever . . . ' hissed Sandra and for a split second, Pat was sure she was going to lose her temper. But it passed, her fleeting moment of irascibility, and by the time it was coming towards three, they had been embracing for so long there, Pat thought he had better do something or he'd be there until morning. And that wouldn't look so good in the quiet, law-abiding town of Dunkeerin! So, adjusting his clothes and his Ben Sherman shirt, Pat coughed and said: 'I think I'd best hit the road, pet. Otherwise I'll never make it.'

At the door, under the porch light, Sandra gave him a last kiss and told him how much she had, first of all, enjoyed the evening, and, secondly, was looking forward to the wedding.

Which made Pat smile as he thought about it now, driving home listening to the radio, and trying to keep his eyes open, which wasn't proving easy. But he'd make it all right, he knew. As he cruised along the avenue of sycamore trees which, since the war started, had been dubbed Rosary Row by Tyreelin folk, because of the number of people who had been attacked and murdered there, Pat didn't give it a second thought. He'd travelled it so often, it never occurred to him to do so. Not even when he saw the lamp swinging to and fro in the darkness up ahead for he knew it was probably just the Ulster Defence Regiment who, although they might give him some annoyance, would only delay him for a couple of minutes at the most and that wasn't going to bother him.

But it wasn't the Ulster Defence Regiment. Although they were, in fact, attired in military dress. But that was just to hoodwink drivers like Pat. Who didn't know what was happening until he received a solid blow form a wheelbrace across the head.

How long he had been awake, Pat didn't have the faintest idea. The problem was that he kept waking and passing out again. Where exactly the garage was—or if it even was a garage—he wouldn't have been able to say, but he felt it was miles and miles away from where he had been picked up. He really wished they would do what he knew they were going to do in the end anyway, because it was as clear as day he was never going to see Sandra again. Which suited them fine, of course, because they didn't like him associating with protestants—or 'their' kind as they put it. After reviving him with a bucket of cold water, they told him that they didn't mind him 'riding taigs' or 'screaming wee Catholic witches' but when it came to clean, God-fearing protestant ladies, they could not stand by and countenance Catholic cocks squirting the poison of Rome into their spotless, untainted vaginas. It just wasn't right. It wasn't right, they said. Whose idea it was to start chipping at him, Pat didn't know. Of all the tortures so far, he would say it was the worst. It turned him into a solid block of flesh, as sculpture they kept tapping away at with seemingly infinite patience. How many wounds—half-inch nicks—were there on his body when they tired of it? Approximately three hundred. Then they brought out the knives—just an eight-inch at first—and carved some lines right down his back—parallel tracks all the way down.

There was a late-night film on the back and white portable so they watched that until he passed out. It was called *A Great Day for Bonzo*. In his fleeting moments of clarity Pat managed to remember his name and imagined himself running with the children and the dog across the lush and rolling fields of the English countryside. In the final, brief seconds before he felt the Magnum placed against his temple, Pat wondered whether he and Sandra would have had a dog. He thought perhaps Sandra might have been against it but they would have agreed in the end.

Perfume: 1,000,000 v. Stench: 0

How wicked to laugh within such dreams but apparently I did! Wallis even told me! 'You were thrashing about like a facking maniac!' he said. 'What was going through your head?'

'Perfume,' I said. 'Perfume to take the smell away! Perfume one million! Stench—nothing!'

'You're a right one you are!' he goes and says then with a smile.

Quite nice in the end, old Wallis was—I think I rather fancied him!

Even sponging my head as off again I silky-floated, tumbling wild from moon to moon, as sweat it rolled (ugh!) and body it jerked and spasmed.

*

'Write it for me,' Terence said. 'Write it as best you can—it'll help me understand.'

Which it obviously did! Help him understand that the best thing he could be doing with himself is applying for a transfer to another hospital, away from this sad nutty fairy!

Chapter Forty-Six

A View from the Hill

Who now finds herself planked upon a smallish mountain in the shadow of which she grew up, eyeing it viciously with narrowed, kohl-rimmed eyes.

It is almost eleven-thirty in Mulvey's Bar, and Dessie Mulvey the owner is at his wit's end trying to clear the house. 'Ah, for God's sake, lads!', he repeatedly cries. 'Do you want to have the guards on me or what!'

As if the guards would come into Mulvey's at that hour, causing trouble! For, as Dessie well knows, they have far too much sense! Why, the last time they came in trying to throw their weight around, it had practically ended in a riot! Especially when the sergeant committed the cardinal sin of saying something cynical under his breath about the IRA, which you just don't do in Mulvey's—because it is a Provisional IRA pub, of course! And more especially still when one of their number who was well known in the bar had been taken into custody by the very same policemen and savagely beaten. It was silly of the sergeant and, almost as soon as he'd said it, both he and his colleagues knew it. But it was already too late, for Jackie Timlin and the Horse Kinnane had risen from their seats and were giving him looks that did not exactly say: 'We understand your predicament, sergeant. If you'll just give us one or two more minutes?'

Only for Dessie's adroitness in playing peacemaker that night, there might have been a lot more broken than the window in the toilets which Horse put his fist through, cursing: 'Pigs! Fucking pigs!' as the golden arc of his urine irrigated practically every spot on the wall in front of him, bar the chipped white section of it marked Armitage Shanks. It was particularly fortunate that they didn't arrive on the scene this evening too because, on account of a new arrival home from Portlaoise prison, where the volunteer had been serving five years for membership of an illegal organisation, spirits were higher than usual, with any number of choruses of 'The Boys of the Old Brigade', 'The Broad Black Brimmer' and the current favourite, 'The Sniper's Promise'.

The volunteer concerned was understandably overjoyed at the welcome he received, for the solitary in which he'd been placed for an attack on a prison officer, had come close to driving him clean daft. As he observed to the Horse and Jackie who had just bought him a triple vodka and were insisting he drank it, 'It's good to be home.' Which prompted Jackie and the Horse to toast: 'Cheers!' after which they lapsed once more into what a keen-eyed observer, whose perceptions were not dimmed by either alcohol or euphoria—as those of the volunteers most certainly were—might have termed 'a sullen silence'. The cause of which no one, apart from themselves, could possibly have known, simply because it wasn't the sort of thing you could tell to anyone, possibly even for as long as you lived. 'It was sad,' ran the thought through Horse's mind, 'having to kill someone.' But particularly when you liked them.

And Horse liked Irwin Kerr, all right. So did Jackie. They had gone to school with his brother. Knew the whole family, for God's sake. But what could they do? Already they had lost three valuable volunteers because of his informing and were likely to lose God knows how many more if it were allowed to continue. Not to mention God knows how many arms dumps. They supposed that he possibly knew what was going to happen to him. All sorts of hints had been dropped by other volunteers (down to 'The Dead March' being hummed one night when he got up to go to the toilets) and he had been warned more directly on a few occasions by Jackie. 'If they are putting pressure on you,' he'd said to him, 'the cops—whoever. . . . tell us. Tell us, OK? Don't let it go until it's too late.'

But he had and now he was going to die. Jackie and the Horse truly wished the job had been given to someone else but they were both the top local men so that was that. They decided to have one more drink. 'Before the cops come!' they laughed, and then headed out to Cardonagh Lake where the job was to be done.

It was a beautiful night—an unblemished moon hanging over the steely water like a child's wondrous toy. What made it worse was that when Irwin arrived—or the *'tout'* as they forced themselves to call him now—he insisted on cracking stupid jokes as if they'd all gotten together to go on a fishing trip. 'Did you hear about the Cavan man who went on holidays. . . ?' As Jackie barked: 'Shut up!'

After they had tape-recorded his confession, they put the black plastic refuse back over his head and brought him off.

By now he was wetting himself and defecating. Jackie was on the verge of getting sick as he took out the pistol. Horse looked away when he did it and out of nerves Jackie attacked him. 'I thought *you* were going to do it!' he screamed. The trickle of blood mixed with the sound of the water lapping as he tried to drown it out with even more shouting. What he was dreading was lifting Irwin and putting him in the boot, having to drive to the quarry to dump him, which was why he cried out again and started flailing at the air and clutching his throat as if for him too now the stench was no longer bearable.

Die, Daddy!

Which it certainly was for Puss and now upon her prison settlebed she shrieked: 'I've come for you! You see I've come for you at last and you're going to pay now! Just like *him*, you're going to pay!'

Meaning Father Bernard, of course, her own dear father whom she could not forgive!

'You're going to die, Daddy!' she squealed. 'You and all of you who brought poison to the valley! I'm going to burn your church with you inside it! You think I won't! But I will, you see, I've got all night and till I'm finished I won't stop!'

Chapter Forty-Seven

Vicky Likes Salmon!!

A wicked fairy squealing as havoc she would most definitely wreak! But nonetheless a little nervous now as Big Vicky opened the door and stood back to view his visitor. 'O pray God that I look luscious!' Pussy said to herself and raised her skirt a tiny bit. Big Vicky was the only one looking at her because the others were to busy cleaning up the mess after their torture victim had expired—not Pat McGrane, but a neighbour who lived not far away from him, in fact. And, as usual, they were cursing and complaining about all the hosing and whatnot they had to do each and every time they went out on a job. They were still at it when Vicky drew his flak-jacketed arm across his mouth and sank his tongue in his cheek as he said: 'Say, boys. Looks like we've got a visitor.' Now it really was a wise precaution for a cute little Pussy to have chosen the most expensive underwear one could find because you could tell by the exasperated comments regarding the tiresome nature of the night's work that these were men whose patience could be tried very easily ('Fucking Big Vicky! Fucking, fucking Big Vicky—always ordering us about!') and Pussy didn't want that, ending up being

171

hung from the rafters by the tootle with all those nasties poking blades into her pale white flesh!

I was so pleased Vicky was fond of salmon pink. 'I wore it specially for you,' I said and give him a mischief-smile. 'But we can only play in private! Sweet Puss is shy,' I said.

And did Big Vicky's eyes go—jump—or what! As he winked at all his tattooed friends and led Puss by the hand to show he his big pistol.

Which he did! O! And did she get excited!

'Gosh! It's such a great big gun! She gasped as she saw it peering out from behind his great big army jacket. 'What is it?' she enquired meekly, for she knew nothing at all about guns. As she informed him with her finger in her mouth.

And which he was ever so glad to hear, he said, because he'd tell her all about it. 'Oops. Look! Your tootle is hanging down!' thought Puss but didn't dare to say it—for Big Red he might not like it! All of a sudden, maybe, go and shoot poor whoopsies in the doo-do! But no—he's too busy taking it out—his great big gun, of course! and stroking it like it's the most precious metal in the world and saying: 'Like Dirty Harry says—it's a Magnum, and it's the most powerful handgun in the world. You want to see what it can do to a man's face!'

'Or a girl's face, Vicky-poosy!' Puss says, all shivery-shaky at the thought, then pleading with an eyelash flutter: 'May I?'

'But of course!' says Big Vicky with a wink, meaning: 'But I've got an even bigger one to show you after.'

Which he has, of course, as Pussy well she knows, except that there isn't going to be one, an 'after', that is, as Big

Vicky knows right now, what with Pussy pulling the trigger and making a huge hole in the middle of his disagreeing face. Disagreeing because it is as if he is saying to himself: 'You can say this is happening but I don't agree with you.' Which didn't matter very much anyway because before he had any time to continue the argument with himself, or some person whose face he was imagining inside his head, Pussy had gone and done it again—this time aiming at his you-know-what! And not a bit ashamed! Not in the slightest bit perturbed as she flicked a tiny particle of lipstick into her mouth from the bottom of her lip and said: 'Let's see what you do with it now, Big Darling! Big big darling, Vicky!'

Terence Was Right

(This piece I hate to read because I know Terence was right about forgiveness—and it contains everything he asked me not to feel! But here it is—with old 'Fly-By-Night's' fingerprints all over it. Sorry, Ters. I don't mean that. Why do you think I keep them? If I hated you, I'd have burnt them long ago, along with every memory I have of you. Some chance!)

Chapter Forty-Eight

A Church in Flames

Father Bernard is busy washing his hands, whistling to himself as he wonders: 'Have I got everything now!' for sure as God he would leave something behind him as he did every Saturday night when he went off to the church to hear his confessions—only remembering it, be it his rosary beads or prayerbook or his Silvermints when he was halfway there, having to come all the way back down the hill to the presbytery to get them. 'No,' he mused now, 'I'm nearly sure I have everything with me,' and, wiping his hands on the towel which his housekeeper, Mrs McGlynn (still with him after all these years—her only time away being for a short period in the mid-fifties when—No! No! *Please!*) had delicately, fondly laundered for him as always. Checking his accoutrements one last time—sometimes he hated himself for his fastidiousness—he sighed and, closing the door behind him, set off up the hill to make his way to the Church of the Holy Saviour.

The first penitent he laid eyes upon was Mrs McGivney, a devout woman in her sixties who, God bless her, had never committed a sin in her life greater than harbouring uncharitable thoughts regarding her neighbours. Close by was P. Counihan, a solicitor of advanced years who, in all his time in the town, as far as Father Bernard could remember, had never once missed his daily Mass.

To these two kind people, Father Bernard nodded warmly, appreciatively, before stopping at his confessional and clicking open the door, casually wondering to himself who perhaps the stranger might be, the headscarved woman in the drab overcoat who was kneeling over by the side aisle, praying fervently with her head in her hands. He said to himself as he took up his place inside the box that he must say hello to her before he left—if she was still there, of course.

Which indeed she was! After all, you are hardly going to come all this way to do something and then at the last moment, turn around and not do it. At least, the dark, dreaming Avenger wasn't! Not after all that she'd been through!

Which was why she was giddy as a young goat! Remember—it was the first time she had seen her father since before being expelled from school and going to England! And before that had seen precious little bar the tail of a soutane as it went flapping by, or a shy smile as Daddy quickened his step on the street and thought to himself: 'O no! It's *him*! My twilight zone son! And he's going to come over to talk to me!'

Which begged the question, of course—what did he mean—him?

'What do you mean—*him*?' it was Pussy's plan to say—and then open her coat at that precise moment!

Obviously, it was going to be a little bit of shock! After all, you don't see someone in an old housecoat and headscarf in the mid-fifties and then suddenly meet them again in 1974 sporting check yellow blouses and Mitzi Gaynor Capri pants! Of course you don't!

Is it any wonder he'd cry, poor Father Bernard, 'Who— who on earth are you? And what are you doing in my church?'

*

Which, of course, would be quite enough, for by now and, would you blame her, Puss would have had just about as much of that particular line of questioning as she could bear, not to mention all the: '*What* are you's!' which she'd also to endure. It really was as much as she could be bothered with and why she scratched his face and scratched it again and he cried no no no. 'O no!' she hissed, 'I'm not your son, correct, my father, because what I am's your daughter or hadn't you noticed your gorgeous man in lace and serge, you've passed me on your journeys,' raising her hand to gouge his eye as back across the candle flames he fell and begged for mercy just as 'Ah!', poor Saviour on the cross, now too did plead for some, but none it came I fear, not one scrap was to be found, as out in the night a bad bitch burned and burnt it, his poor church to the ground, with petrol splashing about its doors and into its heart a bluelit taper thrown across the valley all her madness—for what else could you call it now—like a cackling nightbird of the blackest hue took wing, as the flames they licked the sky and in her wild and daring eyes, flesh melted on an old man's bones.

'You fucking bastard!' she squealed, bad gremlin on a fern-furzed hill. 'You fucking fucking bastard! Never will I forgive you! Never never never!'

Chapter Forty-Nine

A Sudden Burst of Gunfire

There is not much happening in Mulvey's. The crowd generally doesn't appear in until nine or thereabouts. Which is why there is no commotion at all apart from the newscaster repeating details of some murders in the north and requesting keyholders in Ballymena to return to their premises. 'Ho hum,' sighs Dessie as he washes the glasses under the tap. As one of the customers put his cigarette to his lips and takes a long, deeply satisfactory drag. Just as the pebbled glass of the front window comes in and a tongue-shaped shard knocks the ciggie out of his hand, almost shearing the side of his cheek off into the bargain. For a moment or two, Dessie is on the verge of saying: 'Ah now, lads! Stop this!' But soon thinks the better of it as a harp in a glass case—fashioned by a prisoner in one of the country's top high-security prisons—falls to the floor and breaks in bits. The customer, still, ridiculously, on the high stool, is thinking to himself: 'What is this—the end of the world or what?' as another burst of gunfire rakes the walls and from outside is followed by a wicked, girlish chuckle. For it is Puss, of course—who else—now retreating in the dark, giddy and sweating all over and sad that she has had to do it—even though she knew she would—watching the Church of the Holy Saviour, as it once was, light up the entire valley, nasty flames so tantalizingly weaving as if to say: 'You weren't expecting this, people of Tyreelin!'

Free!

At which point her eyes snapped open, vengeance totally incomplete! 'O no!' she cries. To find there—Routledge!—with a big tin mug of steaming tea and a beaming smile that said: 'You're free!'

Chapter Fifty

Lynsey de Paul

Which was a bad thing, of course (from now on I think I'll just be honest and write for myself—somehow I have this sneaking feeling my doctor won't be in this morning—ha ha!), because although I did dream a lot of nutty stuff and get real vengeance thoughts and trails of retribution into my head, at least in jail the sedatives weighed me down a little and I didn't feel like I did the very minute I got outside—yes!—stuffed into a ballista and sent rocketing a couple of million miles across the sky with not the faintest idea as to where I was going to land, and worse still, knowing when I go there, my legs would be like string again and there'd be someone there to say: 'What do *you* want here?'

But, try as I might, my protests came to nothing, with the result that Routledge and Wallis, they literally had to push me out of the station, dressed like Gilbert O'Sullivan, the pop singer, in a pile of old ex-prisoner's hand-me-downs they'd found in a locker saying: 'You stay off the game now, you hear us, Pat?'

Which of course they knew I hadn't the slightest intention of doing, not only because I had to earn some fast cash to do myself up a treat (I felt horrible in those rags!) but I think because I was secretly hoping that one of these days I'd look up and there they'd be, Routledge and old Wallis, suddenly bursting into a run and going: 'After him!' dragging me back to prison to make me feel cosy and rooted and snug and always on hand, my two custodians to say: 'Well, at least he can say *we* know him!'

*

As off I went about my business—to ply my trade, in other words—and you should have seen the face of the city gent when he saw me in my trousers!

'Why it's like making love to Charlie Chaplin!' he says and as I took the crisp notes, assuring him I had to agree.

Quite what I was doing entertaining so many baldy chaps to get the money for my fare home to Tyreelin, there is no point in my trying to explain because I was as high as a kite and that was all here was to it! I think my prison dreams had turned my head and I was seriously beginning to think I *was* about to embark on some crazy hallucinatory vengeance trail!

*

One thing *was* certain—I definitely did look a treat, for the fellow who was sitting beside me on the aeroplane (Yes! I said—why not! Blow the ugly ferry! As I'd made an absolute fortune in just one week!) couldn't do enough for me, leaning over nearly every minute asking me was I enjoying the flight and would I like something, another drink perhaps and what did I think of London and God knows what else! What didn't occur to me, so excited was I by everything and the speed with which it seemed to be happening, was that I was long out of the ballista spoon and indeed had been fired a lot higher and further than I had ever dreamt of, even in my giddiest and most anxious moments! For although I knew that the act I was putting on for him, fiddling with rings and batting lashes and so forth, whilst I might have done it in *hotel-room* privacy with a customer, up until then, would never have, in a million years, in public, never never never! (At least I'd had that much sense!) Now I just couldn't sit still, plucking at my nylons, my earrings. And the puckering! Then when he said: 'You know something?' You look just like Lynsey de Paul.' (I had pencilled in a beauty spot!) why it drove me absolutely wild!

Chapter Fifty-One

I Become a Bit of a Busybody!

And why in a way I was possibly the worst person Charlie could have got in with at that particular time, because I was completely—I don't deny it—obsessed with myself—changing my clothes three times a day for heaven's sake, sometimes so busy drawing lip-lines I wouldn't hear a word she said.

But in another way that isn't true—it isn't true at all in fact! Because only for me, she wouldn't have had anyone, never mind a place to stay! Who was it went to the auctioneers and rented out the bungalow? The poor man couldn't believe it when he saw the amount of money I had! The eyes nearly popped out of his head! 'Who do you want it for?' he said, as he counted out the notes. 'Oh, just me and Charlie,' I said, not passing the slightest bit of notice, which I soon regretted when I saw the way he looked at me but fortunately I had the good sense to, straight away, interject: 'Oh—and a few others too—bank girls!'

Which I'm sure he didn't believe, of course—as indeed why should he when it was naught but a pack of lies! I knew no bank girls! But what I did know was that Charlie Kane needed somewhere to live and quick too because if she stayed out any more nights, the silly cow would die of hypothermia!

What happened, you see, was that after Irwin's murder she was so bad she'd missed all her exams—after which there was another furious row with her parents, ending up with her being thrown out of the house. It really is hard to believe that's how it happened, just as it was to believe that the half-scarecrow I'd met tumbling around the village with a bottle of vodka was the same old Charlie I'd known all my life—but it was!

You should have seen the face of her mother when she went down looking for her belongings! She turned as white as a ghost when she saw me and backed off as if I was going to assault her or something. 'Is that you, Patrick?' she said. 'Patrick Braden?' and when I said yes, dropped her voice and said, shakily, but still looking me up and down: 'I'll get them for you.' I just stood there on the doorstep, adjusting my skirt and twisting buttons on my blouse, waiting for her to invite me in—which she didn't!

The best thing I ever did for Charlie was buying her the dog to keep her company because it worked like I knew it would—it really did. He was a little cross-bred terrier (Pomeranian and Jack Russell, they told me) with bat ears that she called 'Squire', after Chris Squire who played bass with Yes, and who, before the wicked bastards killed him, had given her hours and hours of pleasure!

Because that's what they are—wicked! Wicked, wicked, wicked—all of them—to do a thing like that!

No matter, like I said to Terence, what misunderstandings there might have been about Martina Sheridan, and these things can happen—everyone knows they can!—

they're one thing! But to do the like of that—strangle a poor little dog with barbed wire!

Except that, as Terence got me to see—how much I have to thank that man for, I can't begin to tell you—it makes no sense to keep going: '*Them!*'

(Was it the whole town who had it in for you and who arranged to do such a terrible thing to the dog?, he'd said.)

But of course it wasn't! A small minority was responsible for that—the sort of people who weren't happy themselves and seemed to have nothing better to do than dedicate their lives to making sure no one else was either. What is particularly sad is that up to that, myself and Charlie were having an absolute ball—we were having a wonderful time, we really were, living it up on our social security and what remained of my savings! Night, noon and morning I'd spend scrubbing and polishing the place until it was absolutely spotless, then sit down and read my magazines and have my coffee or whatever.

Despite the fact that we were having what I have described as a really good time, it was still very hard to get really what you might call an awful lot of sense out of Charlie because she was still drinking you see and sometimes, to tell you the truth, I would have to go into the bedroom and tell her to turn off the record player, one time actually losing my temper so much I shouted: 'I think we've had enough for God's sake!' after which I was sorry because she looked at me with those hurt, bewildered eyes.

Which means I must have been on edge, I suppose, without realizing it, and maybe, with so much time on my hands—(I mean, most of my housework was done by mid-day)—and did, perhaps, as Terence suggested—and I don't blame him for it because I know he was only trying to help me—become a bit of a busybody.

All I can really remember about those days is sitting there by the window, suddenly seeing a spot on the Venetian blind and running out to get a cloth to clean it and suddenly bursting into tears whenever I took my coffee up again. What this was all about, I hadn't the faintest idea because, as I say, I should have been as happy as Larry—it wasn't as if I'd been through anything like Charlie, having to look at someone I loved with a hole in his head that you could put your fist into. But still I couldn't stop feeling weepy.

Maybe that explains why I couldn't get Martina Sheridan out of my mind. Whether it's all just an excuse and I was using her, taking my weepiness out on her, I don't know. All I know is, I didn't mean to shout at her, or poke my nose into her business. I just wanted to help her. To make her see what she was getting into. I knew Tommy McNamee cared nothing for her. He was a married man and whenever he'd got what he wanted would just leave her there, probably not even remember her name. But she couldn't know that. She was too young, how could she have known? She couldn't understand!

What I am sorry about is that I shook her behind the creamery that day and I know now that I did, I must have because that was why she started crying. I am deeply sorry that that had to happen. Not because it spoiled everything and started the whole commotion about the village but because after that, *I* got excited too and didn't know what I was saying. I was in such a state by the end of it that I am sure my voice was so shrill she didn't know *what* I was saying, so the whole purpose of it was defeated.

'Tommy McNamee's only taking advantage of you!' I kept crying. 'He'll only use you and then leave you! Can't you see that? Why can't you, Martina! Why?'

I was so depressed after that I can't tell you, so bad that even Charlie could see I was worse than her, putting her arm around me and saying it would be all right but I knew it wouldn't be all right, if it was, why were half the young girls of the village going around pushing buggies, with babies they never bothered to wash, never even lifted them out to cuddle once in a while, why because they didn't want them!

'And never did, Charlie, never wanted them in the first place!' I said and started sniffling then, seeing it all as plain as day, the nun making her sign the papers, Martina hardly more than a child herself and the baby, with a tag on its ankle, being taken away from its village and its home (Home? Ha! Where's that, I wonder!) and never be seen again.

It was so predictable that by the time I had the tissue Charlie gave me frittered away to shreds, there was nothing else I could do but hold her wrists so as it would sort of hold me down and say to her: 'O Charlie! Charlie! Charlie Kane! The states I get myself into!'

Chapter Fifty-Two

'I'm in Love!'

Which from the highest rooftops you could loudly cry for every word of it was true, except that where I'd been with tears and giddy walkings through the nights was as nothing to what was about to happen now! Every woman, young girl's longing—that each morning she'll awake to rolling tummy, blinking stars! Each time thinking: 'Oh, but this is silly! It can't be me! It really can't be me!' Only to find, with a swooning so delicious, that not only *can* it, *may* it, but *is*! And *is*! And *is*!

And why I cried: 'At last it's happened! I'm in love! I've found my Home-Loving Man!'

And why I cried: 'At last it's happened! I'm in love! I've found my Home-Loving Man!'

Oh, I know Terence says that I was floating far away and this was the time I should have left Tyreelin village again but he has no idea—he really cannot know what it was like that day it happened, the very first day I felt it in me, shimmering inside like sunlight! Most extraordinary of all is that so many times I'd seen him—strolling about in his denim jacket, loitering about the betting shop, flicking a match to the wind.

But not until that night in Mulvey's, when I felt it in my stomach, turning, tumbling, rolling around, had I ever dreamed it was meant to be. What encouraged me most was that I knew *he* noticed *me*—even though I was wearing only a simple brown suede skirt, black ribbed tights and a pink, lambswool cardigan with some flowers on the front. I had asked Charlie to come down with me but she was so far gone I couldn't get a word out of her so I just said: 'Oh, Charlie! Bother you then!' and went off about my business.

I was so excited after it happened that when I got home, I woke Charlie up and couldn't stop my heart thumping as I cried: 'It's happened, Charlie! At last, it's happened! It's happened! I'm home! Home!' as I climbed in beside her and hugged her and hugged her and hugged her and sang: 'Up on the moon/We'll all be there soon/ Watching the earth down below/ We'll visit the stars/ And journey to Mars/ Finding our breakfast on Pluto!' and then crying 'Charlie! I'm so happy!'

As I lay there with the moon on the window and my fingers entwined with Charlie's, I couldn't stop thinking about him as he got up off his stool to go to the gent's, his keys rattling on his belt and he scratched his big dark sideburns and tossed back his head to laugh at some joke that his drinking pal had just told him. 'My Huggy Bear,' I lay there repeating (that was his nickname—from *Starsky and Hutch*—because he was so big and tall!) to myself the whole night long.

By the time morning came, I had my nails bitten down to the quick and no sooner was I out of bed than I was over at the wardrobe bundling out slips and dresses, already in a right state in case I'd have the wrong thing on if I met him!

Chapter Fifty-Three

If I Wasn't There

I had a row about all this with Terence because he kept saying that I should have realized there would be trouble, that people weren't going to forget the Martina episode so quickly, which was true I suppose, but you see, when you're in love you don't think about these things and that's what Terence will *never* understand! Because he's never *been* in love! Hasn't a clue what it's like to wake up feeling like the lightest feather about to be blown and buffeted away by the most beautiful breeze imaginable! And upon which you will be borne for as long as the love you share with the person you have ever been closest to in your life is destined to last. Which, in my case, wasn't very long, I'm afraid! Three days in fact! Three whole blooming days! I'm nearly sure I saw Terence smiling as I released that little detail to him! God, how embarrassed I am to admit it!

Which had happened, you see, was that after the first night I saw Brendan Cleeve (that was his real name) noticing me—I mean, I didn't imagine it—I *definitely* saw him looking at my legs—well, I'm afraid nothing else happened. And, goodness knows, it wasn't for the want of trying on my part—for I was in there every night after six o'clock. More than prepared to endure the semi-intoxicated, wearily predicable asides of the regulars ('*Look! There she is! Nice to see you to see you nice! Ooh! Shut that door!*) in the hope that he might turn up.

Which he usual did—but not to say anything to me! As a matter of fact, if I'm honest about it, the only conclusion you could draw from his behaviour was that he was going out of his way to humiliate me. How many times I smoothed back my hair and smiled in his direction I don't know. All I know is he looked through me as if I wasn't there.

I suppose I have to admit that, as Terence says, after all I had been through in England and all the silly things I'd done and been thinking about, I really must have been in more of a state than I thought I was (Can you imagine climbing up the highest ladder in the world and having the ladder taken away?) or I wouldn't have done what I did, started sobbing on that third night I mean, not the other thing.

Chapter Fifty-Four

The Other Thing

The other thing—(burning the church? No! I was so happy I'd gone and completely forgotten all about that!)—was unforgivable and if I ever see Tina Kelleher again, I will apologize to her with all my heart, for it was a horrible thing to do, horrible, and only a bitch would do it and I have to admit that as I sat there in Mulvey's, bleary-eyed with gin thinking: 'He's ignoring me again', that that's what I'd become, a bitch and there is no other honest way of describing it. It's just that somehow I'd managed to work it all out so perfectly in my mind, with him and me together at last in the house I'd always dreamed of, our *Chez Nous* picture on the wall ('this is our little home') with its lovely twining flowers and everything spotless for him when he'd come home from work, putting his arms around you with a sort of definite-ness that said: 'You belong here! Here and nowhere else! Instead of brown glass marble eyes that bored right through you and said: 'Who are you?' No! Said: 'Who or *what* are you?'

Which I knew some of them were saying, was sure of it, ever since the Sheridan incident, for there were places— even the supermarket, believe it or not—where conversations would stop dead whenever you walked in. I'm afraid it just shows you how far away I was when only the night before it happened I'd been feeling all warm and cosy sitting there as I thought: 'Well, at least that's one thing Brendan Huggy-Bear will never think.'

And then it happened—those marble eyes they went right though me as if I was in the way of a photo or sign he was trying to read on the wall. I know it doesn't excuse what I did and if I hadn't been so nervous after it and so upset, I don't think, no, I'm sure I never would have done it. I would have drunk up and gone out into the fresh air to clear my head and that's what I will say to Tina Kelleher if I ever see her again, by accident on the street or wherever.

I knew she had been talking to him and I didn't really mind that—I mean, a person's allowed to talk to someone, for God's sake!—and whether or not it was actually her moving her stool in alongside his that did it or touching his arm before their lips met, I couldn't actually say. I have tried to remember *exactly* for Terence but all that really comes back is a sort of blurry picture of me looking down (from miles above!) on this girl—who is *me*!, of course—leaving her seat by the wall and slowly moving across the bar floor, smiling with a funny look in her eye. It seems to take an age as everyone just goes on doing what they're doing, watching telly, ordering drinks, arguing political points—and nobody really realizing what's going on until someone shouts: 'Jesus Christ! Tina! Your hair's on fire!' and after that, everyone shouting as they tried to dampen it with towels, and Brendan looking at me in a way, as I said to Terence, I shall never forget as long as there's breath in my body.

Chapter Fifty-Five

We Leave Tyreelin for Ever

It was after that my dresses and things were stolen from the washing line. (I don't blame Brendan—I think it might have been Smigs and Martina Sheridan's brother—I saw them hanging around the bungalow earlier that day.) They were dumped in the garden a few days later, ripped up and destroyed with all sorts of obscenities scrawled on them in lipstick. But I didn't mind that. I was so far gone, after I realized what I'd done to Tina, that somehow it didn't really register with me at all. It was only when I found Squire that I broke down once and for all, for what they'd done to him was horrible. I knew for sure it was Smigs and Sheridan that time for the next day when I was coming down the street, they wolf-whistled and shouted: '*Woof! Woof!* after me.

I had to concoct a short about him (Squire) running away and even went out looking for him with Charlie for I knew it would break her heart. I think she must have sobbed so much that night as we lay in one another's arms, she sobbed enough for a thousand deaths. If you were to pinpoint the moment of Charlie's gradual recovery, I think it would have to be then—and if by now she'd suffered it all and there was no other way she could go.

One the morning of the day we left, we went to visit Irwin's grave—directly across from Pat McGrane and Eamon Faircroft's—and after talking for a while about the nights in Cavan and how they'd been going to have Rob Strong and the Plattermen playing at their wedding, she described what it was like seeing his face in the morgue and what it had done to her. And that was the last time I ever heard her cry, that day in the graveyard in 1975 before we left Tyreelin for ever.

Chapter Fifty-Six

He's Ours!

Which is a long time ago now, of course, although as I'm sure you've gathered, things haven't changed very much Chez Pussy, I'm afraid, still here moaning and groaning away about all these people leaving her—but with Terence, I honestly just could not believe it! I mean, I actually said to the nurse: 'I've written some stuff I think Doctor Terence will find interesting, nurse,' and what does she say—without batting an eyelid, I swear it's true—'Oh, that doctor won't be coming in any more!' For a while—a minute or so—I just remember standing there, waiting for her to grin and go: 'Ha ha—fooled you, Mr Braden! Here's the doctor coming now!'

But when I looked again she was gone and there was nothing, only the empty corridors and some cries drifting in from a cricket match being played somewhere at the back of the building. As you can imagine, I bawled my eyes out and was in such a state when I went home (they take me as an outpatient now) I was on the verge of burning everything I'd written for him and everything to do with him.

Now that time has passed, however, I'm glad I didn't, because I still do love him in a strange and special way.

Just as I do anyone who takes me in his arms and says: 'Pussy? You do know something, don't you? You know that you and I are going to make our home in this world together, don't you?' Which I most certainly do—except that it never happens!

It happened to Charlie, though, and, if you saw her now, I think she actually looks younger than she did then! Her skin is as fresh as a daisy and even though she had three kids she's still as mad as ever. Not in *that* way, though—the bad way, I mean! No, ever since she met Doug—he was an art student in the Slade college the same time as her, she's become her old self again and nothing gives me greater pleasure than to her the bell going and the sound of all their voices outside.

*

I never did find Mammy, though, despite the fact that after leaving Tyreelin I had the entire city of London scoured looking for her. My escort work I gave up yonks ago, one night just breaking down in the arms of some poor unfortunate man, going: 'Let go of me! You don't love me! None of you love me!' and the next day presenting the Kilburn War On Want shop with the entire contents of my delicious wardrobe! Except for my housecoat and headscarf, of course, which provide so much amusement around this home for tufty-nosed labourers. I was coming in from the shops the other day and ran into a few of them on the stairs. 'Ah, there you are, Mrs Riley!' one of them shouts as another whispered: 'Wired to the fucking moon!'

It was all I could do not to answer: 'Sorry to disappoint you, boys! Wrong planet, I'm afraid!' but then I thought—

what's the point, and just turned the key and came inside. Because the truth is that they really don't bother me much, only when they're drunk or bored and looking for something to do. Once or twice they even asked me to their parties! And definitely got me going again, there's no point in denying it, as I sat there thinking of me swanning down the stairs, flapping my skirts and bursting into their flat, reeking of Chanel, and giving them a Dusty or Lulu performance their innocent little Sligo/Leitrim souls would not be likely to forget in a long time!

But in the end I declined, for that's all over now, let's face it, and all I really want is to be left alone here, flicking through my magazines—*Picturegoer, Screen Parade, New Faces Of The Fifties*—looking yet again for Mitzi and that old bubble-cut of hers, maybe one day taking the time to write it down for Terence, what my fondest wish would be (he asked me to—even though he'll never see it now)—to wake up in the hospital with my family all around me, exhausted after my ordeal maybe, but with a bloom like roses in my cheeks, as I stroke his soft and tender head, my little baby, watching them as they beam with pride, in their eye perhaps a tear or two—who cares!—hardly able to speak as they wipe it away and say! 'He's ours.'

Acknowledgments

'*We Can Work It Out*'. Words and music by J. Lennon and P. McCartney. © Copyright 1965. Northern Songs. Used by permission of Sony/ATV Music Publishing Ltd. All Rights Reserved. International Copyright Secured.

'*Breakfast on Pluto*'. Words and music by Don Partridge and Alan Young. © Copyright 1969. Onward Music Ltd. 11 Uxbridge St London W8 7TQ. Reproduced with kind permission.

'*Windmills of Your Mind*'. Words and music by Michael Legrand and Alan & Marilyn Bergman © Copyright 1968. EMI Catalogue Partnership/EMI Unart Catalog Inc USA/ Warner Bros Reproduced by permission of IMP Ltd.

'*Dancin' on a Saturday Night*'. Words and Music by Barry Blue & Lynsey de Paul. © Copyright 1973. Sony/ATV Music Ltd. All rights reserved. International Copyright secured.